THE FORGET-ME-KNOT

Sheriff Francis Hood Book Three

RICHARD F. MCGONEGAL

THE

FORGET-ME-KNOT

Sheriff Francis Hood Book Three

RICHARD F. MCGONEGAL

A Cave Hollow Press Book

Warrensburg, Missouri 2023

Cave Hollow Press

304 Grover Street

Warrensburg, MO 64093

Formatting and cover design by Stephanie Flint

Cover Stock Images from DepositPhotos

Library of Congress Control Number: 2022945945

Paperback Edition ISBN-13: 978-1-7342678-2-2

To my parents,

Harold Francis Joseph and Helen Rose Guoth McGonegal,

for everything

CHAPTER 1

Sheriff Francis Hood swung a rubber mallet and drove a wooden stake into the spongy soil.

Attached to the stake was a sign that read "Re-elect Sheriff Hood" in white block letters on a blue background.

He stepped back and studied the campaign sign, assessing its placement on the lawn of the ranch-style house in a middle-class subdivision in southern Huhman County, Missouri. Satisfied, he walked to the family van, opened the rear cargo hatch and laid the mallet beside the collection of yard signs.

Following days dominated by late June thunderstorms, the rising temperature and high humidity draped him like a damp shroud. He took a towel from the van's hatch and wiped sweat from his forehead.

On days like today, he reminded himself that although he hated campaigning—distributing pamphlets door-to-door, working a booth at county fairs and parish picnics, placing yard signs—he loved his job and wanted to keep it.

He unfolded a list of names and addresses of supporters who had agreed to display signs. As he ran a finger down the page, his cell phone rang. The screen indicated the caller was his daughter, Elizabeth.

"Hello," he answered.

"Daddy, we found an arm." The words, coupled with her breathy tone of disbelief, assured him he had heard her correctly.

"A person's arm?"

"We think so. It's just a bone, but we looked it up on our phones and it said human."

"Where are you?"

"By the Trestle."

Hood knew the location, which was northwest and nearer the county line. The aging train trestle spanning Cooper Creek was a rusted remnant of the abandoned Missouri, Kansas, Texas (MKT) rail line. The riverbank below, along a tributary of the Missouri River, was a popular gathering spot for teens. "You said we. Who's we?"

"Claire and me and some other kids who were here when we got here."

"I'm on my way," Hood said. "Ask everyone to stick around. I'll want to talk to them."

"Okay."

Hood disconnected and headed for the site. He was disconcerted, as much by his daughter's presence at the Trestle as by the discovery of a detached arm bone.

He focused on the find. The only active missing person report involved James Bishop, owner of the *St. Gotthard Tribune,* which served Huhman County. Bishop had disappeared in August—more than ten months ago—after telling his wife he planned to visit a possible site to build a new printing plant.

Hood's initial investigation had sputtered. Although Bishop's abandoned car was at the site, no body was found, no evidence suggested foul play, and no witnesses or viable suspects emerged. The members of Bishop's immediate family shared a common alibi that they were together when the patriarch disappeared. The loose ends and lack of leads unsettled Hood. Despite his refusal to designate it a cold case, he relegated it to inactive status.

Although the discovery of the bone suggested a possible break in the case, Hood told himself to avoid speculation, particularly since the Trestle was more than 10 miles from where Bishop reportedly disappeared.

As he neared the turnoff to Schoolhouse Road, an image of his 15-year-old daughter at the Trestle wormed its way into his thoughts. The site was typically benign during the day, when teens congregated to gab, horse around, and cool off in the river. In the evenings, however, the Trestle—a proper name in local lore—became a haven for keg parties, pot smoking, sexual activity, and more.

Hood trusted Elizabeth, a rising sophomore at Huhman County R-1 High School. She was a good, but not straight-A, student. And although she seemed sensible and popular, Hood knew teenage angst wasn't always obvious to parents, even to conscientious parents who tried to remain involved in their children's lives.

Hood considered himself a concerned father, but he was not oblivious to the damage his alcoholism had inflicted on his family.

Less than two weeks ago, Hood's wife, Linda, and their daughter had moved back to the family home after a separation of nearly eleven months. Hood had accepted responsibility for the separation. He was not trying to be noble; he was simply being honest.

His program of recovery emphasized honesty. Before the separation, Linda had warned him she couldn't stay with him if he continued drinking every evening until he blacked out, passed out, or both. "It's not that I don't love you," she had said. "I just can't continue to watch you do this to yourself."

The warning wasn't enough. He had tried to hide his drinking, but she knew. He vividly recalled the day—July 26 of last year—when he returned home from work and found his wife and daughter had moved out. He called Linda immediately, arguing, cajoling, and pleading with her to return, but to no avail. After she disconnected, he drank himself into a two-day stupor that ended when he awoke on the kitchen floor—apparently he had passed out while crawling to the liquor cabinet—and decided he had hit his bottom.

He began a program of recovery and had learned much about himself during his eleven months of sobriety. He thought he had embraced the principles of acceptance and tolerance, but now that his family had reunited, he found those principles easier in theory than in practice—particularly as they applied to Elizabeth.

As he turned onto Schoolhouse Road, he refocused on the present. He followed the county road for roughly two miles before turning onto a gravel lane marked only by a crooked, wooden sign hand-lettered with the word: Trestle. The rutted road surface triggered an annoying clatter of yard signs in the back of the van. The racket continued as he drove through a wooded area, finally ceasing when he parked beside other vehicles in a clearing overlooking the river. Looming above was the arched, iron structure rooted in stone pillars and supporting the plank decking and railroad track spanning the river.

As he stepped from the van, Elizabeth and Claire approached, followed by Claire's golden retriever, Alexandra—Alex for short. Elizabeth held a bone in her outstretched hands. About a half dozen other teens—some strangers, some familiar to Hood—gathered in a semicircle around them.

Hood opened the van's hatch, unfolded a clean towel, took the bone from his daughter, and laid it carefully on the cloth. He examined the appendage, which appeared to be an upper arm bone stripped of flesh, muscle, and tissue. He folded the towel to cover it, then closed and locked the van's hatch. "Who found this?" he asked.

"Actually, Alex found it," Elizabeth answered. She told her father they came to the Trestle to walk the dog along the footpath that ran parallel to the river. During the walk, Alex ran into the woods and, when she reappeared, she was carrying the bone in her mouth.

Hood asked if any of the other teens participated in the walk and was told they had not. They learned of the discovery only after the two girls and the dog returned to the clearing.

"Okay. Listen up," Hood told the group. "I'm not sure what we've got here, but I would really appreciate it if you didn't post anything about this, particularly pictures of the bone, on the internet. Whoever this belongs to has a family, and I'd rather they not find out about it on social media. We don't need a lot of speculation and misinformation out there." Even as he spoke, Hood suspected his caution either was too late or would be ignored.

He called his department and informed his longtime dispatcher, Maggie O'Brien, of the situation. He requested backup and alerted Maggie to await further instructions.

After he disconnected, he turned to Elizabeth and Claire. "Okay. Show me where." Hood followed the girls and Alex, now on a leash, as they retraced their steps along the path. Elizabeth pointed out where Alex had departed from them, her direction—deeper into the woods, away from the creek—and where the dog had rejoined them, carrying the arm. He instructed the girls to remain on the trail while he searched the area where he guessed the dog had roamed. Away from the path, the terrain was treacherous. Tangled deadfall and thorny brambles pulled at his pants legs and threatened to trip him. Reluctantly, he decided to end his cursory investigation.

When they returned to the parking area, Hood's chief deputy, Gus "Wally" Wallendorf, was collecting names and contact information from the teens.

Hood and Wally would provide a study in contrasts for any art student. Contours and musculature dominated Hood's nearly 6-foot, 210-pound frame. His well-fitted uniform simultaneously concealed and suggested powerful biceps, forearms, thighs, and calves. His round head was topped with short, sandy brown hair, and an almost perpetual smile dominated his face. Wally, however, was all sharp lines and angles. At 6-foot, 4-inches tall, he was lanky and sinewy, with thin lips, narrow eyes, and unruly brown hair. Both had attended Huhman County R-1 where Hood, now age 46, had graduated two years before his chief deputy.

After Wally finished questioning the teens, Hood told them to go home. He encouraged them to talk with their parents and repeated his futile plea about posting on social media.

As they dispersed, Hood called his wife and told her what had happened, including their daughter's involvement. Then he guided Wally to the van, unlocked and opened the hatch, and unfolded the towel covering the arm.

Wally examined it. "Any ideas?" he asked his boss.

"I'm thinking it belongs to James Bishop, but this is nowhere near the site where his wife and children said he was going and where we found his car."

"Maybe he lied to them," Wally said.

"Maybe he met somebody and they came here," Hood said.

"Maybe someone killed him and moved the body."

"Or cut up the body and scattered the parts."

"Lots of possibilities," Wally said.

"We're getting ahead of ourselves," Hood said. "We don't even know if this is Bishop's arm."

"So, what's the plan?" Wally asked

"Stay here and coordinate with Maggie to assemble a search party. We may be in for a long night." Hood opened the driver's door of the van. "And ask Maggie to put together a press release," he added. "Just the basics."

"Where're you headed?"

"First, I'm going to deliver the bone to Loeffelman," Hood said, referring to the county medical examiner. "Then I'm going to notify Bishop's wife. I know better than to think this will stay quiet very long."

CHAPTER 2

"Humerus," Loeffelman said, as Hood unwrapped the towel to reveal the bone centered on the stainless-steel table in the medical examiner's lab.

Although Hood was aware of Loeffelman's propensity for dark humor, he stared at the medical examiner as if he had uttered blasphemy. "What?"

"Not humorous, o-r-o-u-s," Loeffelman replied. He grabbed Hood's biceps. "Humerus, e-r-u-s, as in upper arm bone."

"Oh," Hood said, relieved. The sheriff saw Loeffelman as a cubist version of the human form. The medical examiner's rectangular face and square jaw sat atop block-like shoulders. His dark eyes were accentuated with bushy black eyebrows, and his head was topped with curly, black hair highlighted with wisps of silver.

"So where did this disarming find come from?" Loeffelman asked.

"In a wooded area along Cooper Creek—near the Trestle."

Loeffelman nodded. "What else do you know?"

"Not much right now. I need some information to go on. I'm guessing it belongs to James Bishop. That's the only active missing person case we've got. Remember he—"

"That's speculation," Loeffelman said, his tone dismissive.

"Any other factual information?"

"No."

"What would you like to know?"

"If it's Bishop's, for starters. How long it's been out there. Anything you can tell me."

"I'll need a little time to do a thorough examination. I'll also need to start the process of obtaining Bishop's medical records. That may—"

"I'm going by the Bishop estate as soon as I leave here," Hood said. "I don't want Bishop's wife to learn about this through social media. Would it help if I asked Marjorie to release her husband's medical records to you?"

"Could speed things up," Loeffelman said.

"Okay, I'll be in touch."

Hood eased the van toward the wrought iron, double gates and stopped. A brick wall extended from each gate along the perimeter of the property as far as Hood could see. An invasive vine had scaled the brick, its tendrils reaching toward a camera, which was perched on the wall and focused on his vehicle. Beside his window was an intercom affixed to a metal post.

He rolled down the window, but before he could press the button and speak, a disembodied voice asked, "May we help you?"

"It's your sheriff, Francis Hood."

"Hello, Francis. This is Anne. From high school, remember?"

"Sure." He hadn't anticipated any of the children would be present. He hoped, particularly, Anne's younger brother, George, would not be. George made no secret that he blamed the sheriff for being either too inept or too apathetic to solve his father's disappearance. "I'm here to see your mother. I won't take much time," he added, as if an apology for the unannounced visit was expected.

"Come ahead," Anne said. The gate opened, producing a persistent squeal.

As the van ascended the serpentine drive, the manicured grounds and stately Tudor home came into view.

Hood's interest in local history was minimal, but he knew the house had been built by Charles Bishop, who was among the early land speculators and developers in Huhman County. Ownership had been passed down through generations to James and Marjorie, who had raised four children here. Hood had no idea which of them was the designated heir to the property or, for that matter, to the *St. Gotthard Tribune*, the family-owned independent newspaper.

Hood parked in the courtyard. As he exited his cruiser, Anne emerged from a side door and stood on a landing at the top of the fieldstone steps.

"Hello Francis," she greeted.

"Hello," he said. "It's been awhile." He climbed the steps, feeling a loose stone wobble beneath his feet.

"More than twenty-nine years—May 18, 1991, to be exact."

Hood noticed her gaze became vacant as she seemed to fixate on something within.

"It was a Saturday night," she continued, "and we were at Nancy Jacobs' high school graduation party. A lot of us graduating seniors were there. Her parents had a pool and they went all out. They even hired a rock band, Golgotha, because Nancy had a crush on the drummer, Kenny Schaefer. I came with some girlfriends. I could tell you their names and what they were wearing, but it's not important. You wore black swim trunks with red and yellow stripes on the side and a black T-shirt with a Queen logo."

Hood was awed and fascinated by her recall, just as he had been when they first shared classes in high school. "I see you still have that memory thing," he said. "What's it called again?"

"Hyperthymesia—also called Highly Superior Autobiographical Memory."

"I remember you said it's pretty rare."

"You have a good memory," she said, a trace of banter in her tone. "It's very rare."

"I just remember our classmates lining up to ask you stuff during study hall and after school."

"Which is ironic," she said. "My nickname was 'brainy Annie,' but I really wasn't that smart. I didn't have any special problem-solving ability. In high school, I struggled with trig and calculus. A lot of students got better grades. But, since elementary school, I've had incredible recall of my own experiences."

In addition to her uncommon memory, Hood noticed Anne also had retained the striking appearance that had characterized her youth. Her long, chestnut hair was simultaneously stylish and casual, her dark brown eyes reflected intensity and depth, and her smile was playfully insouciant.

Anne had dated only sporadically as a student and—now in her mid-40s—was divorced following a marriage in her mid-20s that had lasted less than two years. Hood understood how men could be intimidated by her disarming combination of intellect and beauty—a supposition based on his own emotions in her presence.

"Is your mom home?" Hood asked.

"She's inside. You're lucky. She's having one of her good days today. Follow me."

Hood removed his hat and trailed her into the front entry, speculating—based on Anne's comment—that her mother was suffering some degree of dementia. He purposely tried to match Anne's brisk pace, while quickly surveying the aging grandeur of his surroundings, which included a sweeping, rounded staircase, large portraits, and a free-standing sculpture.

Anne opened double doors to a well-furnished room where Marjorie sat on an Oriental rug and wrestled a Pomeranian puppy for control of a leather chew toy. Hood generally liked dogs—particularly those with a purpose—herders, retrievers, hounds. He was less fond of the toys—poodles, pugs, chihuahuas—which he considered annoying yappers.

He focused on Marjorie. A plastic surgeon obviously had worked on her facial features, which showed none of the crow's feet, marionette lines, or turkey wattle common among women in their 70s. Her taut skin and stylish brunette bob—without a hint of gray—struck Hood as a desperate attempt to preserve a youthful appearance.

"Thank you for seeing me," he said.

"Of course," Marjorie said. "This is Danielle," she added, as she gestured toward the pom with one hand and, with the other, gripped a sofa arm and arose with some effort. At her invitation, they sat on matching sofas facing each other. Danielle jumped into Marjorie's lap and Anne sat beside them.

The demeanor of mother and daughter reminded Hood that the Bishop women always seemed naturally courteous and at ease, in contrast to the Bishop men, who always seemed to be angling for some advantage.

"I wanted to tell you," Hood began, "before you heard it from some other source, that we found an arm bone earlier today in a wooded area where the old railroad trestle crosses Cooper Creek. I don't want to make any assumptions, but I wanted to give you a heads-up before you saw it on the news or social media."

"An arm?" Anne asked, as if confirming she had heard him correctly.

"Yes," Hood said. "We'll know more after Loeffelman, the medical examiner, has a chance to look at it." He turned to Marjorie. "He asked, by the way, if you could arrange to release your husband's medical records to him." Hood fidgeted with his hat. "You know, for identification."

"Identification?" Marjorie asked. Confusion clouded her expression.

"Yes," Hood said. "We're trying to identify who—"

"They're trying to determine," Anne interrupted, addressing her mother, "if it's Father's arm."

"Well," Marjorie said, her tone certain. "It can't be."

Hood remained silent, reluctant to contradict her.

Anne faced the sheriff. "Did you say the arm was found near *the* Trestle—the one on the west side?"

"Yes," Hood said.

"I think what Mother means," Anne explained, "is Father said he was planning to look at a site on the east side. That's where you found his abandoned car. That's where you focused your search."

"I understand that," Hood said. "Right now, I have no explanation. I'm just exploring possibilities. We've got a search under way in the area where the bone was found."

"Well, it can't be my husband's," Marjorie repeated.

"Mother," Anne said. "The sheriff's just trying to figure out whose it is. If Father's medical records eliminate him, that'll help narrow things down."

"I suppose it's all right. Is it all right with you, dear?" Marjorie asked her daughter.

"Of course," Anne said. She faced Hood and added, "I'll help her arrange it."

"Thank you." He waited until the ensuing silence indicated the conversation was over, then added, "Well, if there's nothing else, I'd better go check on how the search is going."

"I'll see you out," Anne said.

Hood followed Anne as they retraced their route to the outdoor landing, where they paused.

"Please keep us updated," Anne said. "The disappearance has taken a toll on Mother. I know she's lonely and, lately, she's been suffering some memory loss."

"Is she all alone in that big house?"

"She has Connie, who comes in on weekdays. She does the cooking and cleaning. I'm usually here on the weekends, particularly on Sunday when I prepare the family dinner." She looked across the grounds into the distance. "Still, it's been difficult for her, the not knowing. It's been difficult for all of us."

Hood nodded.

Anne looked directly at the sheriff. "Anyway, it was good to see you again. Maybe we can have coffee sometime. Get caught up."

"Sure." Although Hood was intrigued by the prospect of "getting caught up" with Anne, he dismissed the invitation as a mere courtesy.

After he left, Anne returned indoors and sat on the rug beside her mother, who had resumed playing with the puppy.

"Do you think we should tell him?" Marjorie asked.

"It's up to you," Anne said.

"I think it's time."

"I'll do it if you want," Anne said, "but we'll need to notify my brothers first so they're not caught off guard."

Marjorie nodded. She released the leather chew toy and the puppy backed up, triumphantly shaking the object clenched in its jaws.

CHAPTER 3

Hood heard the familiar piano melody—his daughter's latest lesson—as he entered the front door. He continued to the living room, where he found his wife nestled in her favorite chair and reading the newspaper.

"How's Elizabeth?" he asked.

"We talked about it when she got home. She seems fine." Linda folded the newspaper section and laid it in her lap. "She's practicing now."

Hood nodded.

"I saved some leftovers for you, but you said Maggie was going to bring pizzas for the search party after her shift ended."

"She did and I'm full." Hood patted his stomach. "I'm going to talk to Elizabeth." He left the living room and headed for the den, where the piano was located.

Although the surface of his marriage to Linda seemed similar to the way it was before their separation, Hood was aware of a deeper undercurrent. In many ways, he sensed they were forging a new relationship rather than modifying an earlier one. The reunification of his family, like his program of recovery, was a process of transformation. He was exploring new paths and he was uncertain of the terrain and where they might lead. He knew he was approaching both cautiously, groping his way forward, simultaneously fearful of and excited by the prospect of change. He felt most comfortable when he focused on acceptance—what his fellow alcoholics called *life on life's terms*. He also was grateful for Linda's innate ability to trust him. She didn't check on his whereabouts or nag him to attend meetings. She supported his recovery, but didn't try to micro-manage it.

He entered the den, where Elizabeth sat on the piano bench with her back toward him. "Hey you," he said, alerting her to his presence.

She stopped playing and turned. "Hi, Daddy."

"That sounded good."

"It really doesn't yet, but it will. Did you find any more bones?"

"No. We searched until dark. We'll start again in the morning."

"Whose arm do you think it is?"

"We're checking on that," Hood said. "Say, I know it's not every day someone finds something like that, so I just want you to know if you want to talk to me, or your mom—"

"No. Claire and I and some of our friends talked about it. We're okay."

"Okay." He knew pressing the issue would be unwelcome and unproductive, so he returned to the living room and dropped into his recliner. The cushions seemed to envelop and massage his aching muscles. He realized only then how tired he was.

"How's Elizabeth?" Linda asked. She turned a page in the newspaper she was reading and, as always, folded it to remove any creases.

"She seems to be handling it very well. She's becoming a very poised young lady. By the way, I stopped by the Bishops' house today and spoke to Marjorie."

"Any of the children there?" Linda asked. Like her husband, Linda was in the same graduating class with Anne. And, like her husband, although she had never been friends with any of Anne's brothers—Jay, Henry, George, even the foster brother, Julian—Linda was acquainted with all of them—at least by reputation.

"Anne was."

"How is she?"

Hood shrugged. "She seems fine. She still has that memory thing. She remembered the last time she saw me at a graduation party, what I was wearing, even the logo on my T-shirt. It's kind of—what's the word?"

"Disconcerting?" Linda guessed.

"It's just weird."

They lapsed into a comfortable silence. She resumed reading and he replayed his meeting with Anne. He felt flattered by the way she had received him after so many years, not so much that she remembered him—that was a given—but that she had been gracious, friendly even. *Maybe we can have coffee sometime. Get caught up.* In high school, Hood recalled, he had been a face in the crowd. He was not among the brightest students, or the worst. He was not one of the gifted athletes whose names were heard frequently on the public address system at the field or stadium. He did not revel in the banter and laughter at the elite lunch table. But now, after reconnecting with Anne, he felt elevated somehow.

"By the way," Linda said, interrupting his musings, "don't forget we're having Otto and Sarah over for dinner tomorrow. And I know, because Sarah told me, Otto is eager to hear a progress report on the campaign."

Sarah was Linda's younger sister—a recovering alcoholic who Linda had tapped as a resource in an effort to understand her husband's drinking—and Otto was a respected banker who was managing Hood's campaign. During the Hoods' separation, Sarah and Otto initially had taken in Linda and Elizabeth until they moved into an apartment.

"Tomorrow?" Hood asked.

"Yes, tomorrow. Have you seen Grindell's latest ad?"

"No. Do I want to?"

"Here." She arose, handed him an open section of the newspaper, returned to her chair, and perched on the edge of the cushion, eager to gauge his reaction.

Hood stared at the image of Stephen "Steve" Grindell, his challenger in the upcoming Republican primary. At age 65, Grindell was nearly twenty years older than Hood. The photograph, Hood thought, depicted a trustworthy, authoritative man with a penetrating, intelligent gaze. Beneath the picture, bold type read:

Experienced: Steve served in law enforcement for more than 40 years, including eight as a St. Gotthard Police Department Captain.

Committed: In the past four years, violent crime in Huhman County has surged. Steve is committed to making our county a safer place to live, work, and raise your family.

It's time for a change. Elect Stephen "Steve" Grindell—Republican for Huhman County Sheriff.

"Why do they always do that?" Hood asked.

"Do what?"

"Shorten their name when they run for office. Michael is always Mike; Thomas becomes Tom."

"Because it makes them seem more approachable," Linda said. "Besides, Grindell didn't create the ad. I'd be surprised if he even saw it. You know this is the work of George Bishop or his hired gun, Chip Luther."

"I guess." Despite his reluctance to agree, Hood knew Linda was correct. He knew because he was attuned to the county gossip and because Linda remained in touch with members of the county's GOP Central Committee, although she was no longer an officer.

George Bishop had recruited Grindell—plucked the officer from retirement, actually—to challenge Hood in the primary. Hood was convinced George's motivation was a spiteful attempt to remove the sheriff who had failed to solve the disappearance of George's father.

"Did you see today's mail?" Linda asked.

"Not yet."

"You got something from the Republican committee," she said. When Hood moved his recliner to the upright position, she added, "Stay there. I'll get it."

She delivered the letter, returned to her chair, and sat.

Hood opened the envelope and read its contents, which hit him like a gut punch. The visible change in his expression prompted Linda to ask, "What's it say?"

"The committee wants me and Grindell to appear before them to seek an endorsement. That's crazy. The party always endorses the incumbent. It's a given."

Linda scrunched her mouth into a crooked frown. "I heard through the grapevine there might be some dissension about the endorsement."

"From who?"

"I don't want to name names. Besides, the person who told me isn't the one behind it."

"Who is?"

"I just heard there's some disagreement among the members. I was told Mrs. Maupin—"

"That old biddy," Hood huffed. "She hasn't liked me since I was appointed to serve out Westerman's unexpired term," he added, referencing his predecessor, Cliff Westerman. "Good thing I haven't had any primary opposition for the last two terms. How much clout does Mrs. Maupin still carry with the committee?"

"Not as much as she used to, but she's still a force to be reckoned with."

Hood shook his head. "You know how I feel about politics. I don't even know why it's part of the job. I mean, why do we elect a sheriff? We don't elect a police chief or highway patrol superintendent. The city council or the governor appoints someone with the experience and credentials to do the job. That's how the county should be set up. The county commission should be empowered to appoint the sheriff based on qualifications."

"I know," Linda said, "but that's not how it works."

"Well, it should." Hood was warming to the subject. "The whole structure of county government is fouled up. Why do voters elect an assessor, a treasurer, or a recorder of deeds? They're administrators."

"I agree."

"Elections are popularity contests. The most qualified people don't always win. Sometimes, they don't even run."

"I hear you." Linda's tone was calm, designed to cool the fervor of her husband's diatribe. "I know how you feel about running for office, but I have confidence in you."

"Well, I'm glad you do, because mine is fading fast."

"Let's stay positive here," Linda said, her tone upbeat. "You have the advantage of the incumbency. You have name recognition, an excellent record."

"And Grindell has a campaign financed by the Bishops, the wealthiest family in the county, if not all of central Missouri. They could outspend me without having to raise a dime."

"Don't be so sure. The newspaper business isn't the gold mine it once was. The internet and 24-hour news networks have taken a toll. Besides, do you really think Marjorie will loosen the family purse strings for George?"

"I know people think she's a miser, but she has a soft spot for her children."

"Everyone knows that," Linda said. "And everyone knows George is just a spoiled, rich kid trying to buy an election because he's got an axe to grind."

"Plus he's got Chip Luther, who managed winning statewide campaigns for secretary of state and state auditor."

"And you've got Otto Kampeter. He may be my brother-in-law, but he knows almost everybody in Huhman County and is related to half of them. He's smart and capable, and voters will appreciate he's a native who has done a lot for this community."

Hood sighed audibly. "I know all that. I'm just worried."

"I know nothing I say will make you stop worrying, but I'm telling you—not as your wife, but as a voter—you deserve to win. You're the better candidate."

CHAPTER 4

Hood entered the limestone courthouse and descended to the basement, where the offices of the Huhman County Sheriff's Department were identified by a solid oak door emblazoned with a five-point star and black block letters shadowed with gold.

He swiped his security card, entered, and headed for the coffee maker on a counter adjacent to the dispatch station. Although it was early on a Sunday, Maggie, his veteran dispatcher, was on the job.

"Didn't expect to find you here," Hood said. He poured coffee into a disposable cup.

"And good morning to you," Maggie said, the rebuke in her tone unmistakable. "I switched with Heather," she continued, referring to the relatively new hire. "Since we've got a search going on and I'm familiar with the Bishop case, I thought I should be here. Besides, I wanted to retrieve the file on his disappearance. It's on your desk."

Hood appreciated her dedication and efficiency, but was not surprised by it. At age 61, Maggie had anchored the department for nearly two decades before Hood first donned a uniform. In addition to raising nine children, she continued to nurture a gaggle of grandchildren and to serve as the agency's matriarch, counselor, archivist, and more.

He lifted the coffee pot and asked if she needed a "warmer."

"I'm good."

"Anything happen overnight I need to know about?"

"Nothing urgent. Reports are on your desk."

"Okay. I'll be in my office."

Hood navigated among the desks arranged in the open floor plan, entered his office, and left the door open. As usual, incident reports from overnight were stacked neatly beside the daily newspaper Maggie had left on his desk. At the center of the desk was an accordion folder on James Bishop's disappearance.

He kept his office functional and tidy. Clutter distracted him, tempting him to spend time straightening up instead of pursuing investigations. His massive oak desk, like the three mismatched captain's chairs facing it, were antiquated, if not antiques—all handed down by his predecessor, Cliff Westerman.

Hood lowered himself into his chair—an oak swivel chair he had outfitted with a cushion—and opened the folder he hadn't looked at in nearly a year. The contents included notes and tape recordings from the original interviews, which he and Wally had divided between them.

He lifted a page of questions he had written and read: Was Bishop's disappearance voluntary or involuntary? If voluntary, why would a man who seemingly has everything—family, friends, a business, community status, wealth, and more—disappear?

An axiom frequently cited by Matthew, his sponsor in recovery, seemed applicable. If you're troubled, Matthew often said, either you're not getting what you want or you're getting what you don't want. If Bishop intentionally disappeared, Hood asked himself, was it to avoid something, acquire something, or both?

More likely, he considered, Bishop's disappearance was involuntary; he was either kidnapped or killed. If so, who was responsible?

Hood lifted a page of notes he had labeled Fact Sheet, which was based on his initial interview with Marjorie. She said she and her husband traditionally hosted a family dinner at 1 p.m. on Sundays. On the day of the disappearance, the parents and children had gathered at 11 a.m. to consider a proposal to build a new printing plant.

According to Marjorie, the discussion quickly disintegrated into divisiveness and confrontation. She said her husband—who obviously was rankled by the turn of events—stood abruptly and announced he was going for a drive. She followed him to the door and tried to calm him, without success. When she asked where he was going, he said he needed a break from the family argument so he planned to scope out a potential building site on the east side. Before he left, he shouted to the children that he would be back by 1 p.m. and he expected more civil behavior at the dinner table.

When asked for a description of what he wore, Marjorie said he had on a white polo shirt, khaki slacks, and walking shoes. She said he kept a light blue windbreaker and rubber overshoes in his car and may have put the jacket on as well, since the morning temperatures were cool following overnight rains. She added that when he failed to return and efforts to locate him were unsuccessful, Hood was summoned.

Because missing persons cases frequently involve domestic issues, Hood's first order of business had been to create a chart listing the Bishops and their relationships, ages, education, and employment. He located the document and read:

James Bishop, age 73, Owner and Chief Executive officer of the *St. Gotthard Tribune.*

Marjorie Bishop, age 72, wife of James.

Anne Bishop, age 46, daughter of Marjorie by a previous marriage and stepdaughter of James; Bachelor's degree in Accounting from Washington University, St. Louis; Certified Public Accountant (CPA) and newspaper's Chief Financial Officer.

James "Jay" Bishop Jr., age 44, oldest son; Bachelor's degree in Journalism from the University of Missouri-Columbia; Managing Editor at newspaper.

Henry Bishop, age 41, second oldest son, Bachelor's degree in Applied Economics and Management from Cornell University, Ithaca, N.Y.; Advertising Manager at newspaper.

George Bishop, age 39, youngest son; Associate's degree in General Studies from Moberly Area Community College, Moberly, Mo. Newspaper's Production Manager.

In addition to serving as department heads at the newspaper, the four children each held a 12 percent share in the business and served on the board of directors. James maintained a majority, 52 percent, share.

Rereading the chart reminded Hood of his initial impression that the newspaper operation was more than a family business; it was a case study in nepotism. Hood suspected James had groomed each of the children for a specific role—granting or withholding favor, money, even love, as necessary, to ensure his wishes were followed.

He considered how disappointed the patriarch would be to know that, since his disappearance, two of the children had resigned their newspaper posts. Hood updated the chart to reflect Anne's employment as executive director of the Mid-Missouri Foster Care and Adoption Association and Henry's move to Vero Beach, Florida, for a job in musical theater at a performing arts center there.

Also listed on the chart was Julian Beck, 28, a foster child who had lived with the Bishop family for less than a year before he turned 17 and aged out of the foster system. Julian, Hood knew, now lived in adjoining Sterling County. He worked full-time as a mechanic for Checkered Flag Auto Repair, owned by Ed McCullough, and part-time as a sprint car driver for Ed McCullough Racing Inc.

As Hood pondered the chart, he wondered if it would prove more useful than it had during his initial investigation, which evaporated when he learned the family members shared the common alibi—they were together when James disappeared.

Julian had been among Hood's initial suspects. Since

leaving the foster system, Julian gradually had lost touch with the Bishops, with the exception of Anne, who insisted on keeping in contact. But he also had an alibi. After finishing third at Knoxville Speedway in Iowa on the Saturday night before the Sunday disappearance, Julian and his girlfriend, Kim, claimed they had slept in the camper shell of his truck in the speedway parking lot because they were too tired to drive back to Missouri.

All other leads or suspects were tenuous and dissolved under scrutiny, leaving the sheriff with no evidence of a crime and no investigation to pursue.

Hood's musings began to rekindle old frustrations, and he was thankful for the interruption created by his ring tone. The screen indicated the caller was Loeffelman.

"This is your sheriff," Hood answered.

"I've got some preliminary results," Loeffelman said.

"Already?"

"I said preliminary."

"It's Sunday."

"You seemed eager to get information. If you're not interested, I can just as easily pack up and go home."

"No, no. I'm on my way."

Hood exited and crossed an alley separating the courthouse from its annex. Like the sheriff's department, the medical examiner's complex was located in a basement.

Loeffelman greeted Hood and led him into the examination room, where the bone—with its dirt and debris removed—was centered atop the stainless-steel table.

"Keep in mind these are preliminary findings," Loeffelman said, "but they're pretty conclusive." The medical examiner walked to a nearby desk, picked up a manila folder, and handed it to the sheriff. "I found evidence of a prior fracture that's consistent with an x-ray from James Bishop's medical records. All the other proportions match."

Hood took the folder but didn't open it. "So it's Bishop's arm?"

"The odds that someone else would have lost an exact duplicate of Bishop's left arm are astronomical."

"Was it cut off—like with a saw or knife?"

"There are no markings consistent with saw teeth or a knife blade, but absence only proves if the humerus was severed at a joint, the cutter was very careful. The bone itself, however, reveals some information." Loeffelman removed a small metal device from the pocket of his lab coat and extended the telescopic pointer. "Look here," he continued, pointing to a section of the bone. "See those striations? Those were made when the flesh was being torn away by teeth and beaks. A body in the woods is a veritable smorgasbord for scavengers."

Hood produced a guttural noise, indicating his disgust.

"I know," Loeffelman said. "Gross, right? We can only hope, for Mr. Bishop's sake, this occurred post-mortem."

"You don't think—" Hood began, even more repulsed.

Loeffelman shrugged. "If he somehow became immobilized, who knows? We may never know. Finding the body may offer additional evidence, but it may not."

"We're searching the area now for any other remains."

"May I make a suggestion?"

"Of course."

"I don't know the parameters of your search, Francis, but consider an expansive area. An animal or animals could have chewed off this limb and carried it a considerable distance."

"I'll tell Wally to widen the search."

"And tell the searchers to watch for areas that are richer or greener than their surroundings."

"Will do," Hood said, aware nothing was wasted in nature's economy. A decomposing corpse not only fed creatures, it fertilized soil. He glanced at the manila folder he held. "Is this my copy?"

Loeffelman nodded.

"I'll notify Marjorie the bone belongs to her husband," Hood said, "but I'm not going to share the details with her."

"I understand," Loeffelman said. "Also, it's possible Bishop isn't dead. Losing an arm isn't necessarily fatal."

"I think, at this point, offering false hope would be cruel," Hood said.

"Your call."

Three of the Bishop children—Jay, Anne, and George—were seated near their mother at one end of an elongated dining table that seated twelve and could be expanded to accommodate up to eighteen.

After weekly attendance at the family dinner had dwindled from seven to four, Anne had suggested moving to the smaller table in the kitchen, but Marjorie insisted on preserving tradition—understood to be life before her husband disappeared, Henry relocated to Florida, and Julian aged out of foster care.

The clanking and scraping of silverware on plates were the only sounds as the foursome finished the Sunday meal, which Anne routinely prepared.

Although the children at the table considered themselves fortunate to share in the family's bounty, each periodically admired or resented Henry for moving away. More varied and complex were their relationships with Julian.

Those absences left voids, but the disappearance of the patriarch created upheaval. Although hope remained that James Bishop was alive, would reappear, and provide a satisfactory explanation, uncertainty left the family members—and the newspaper's future—in limbo.

As time passed, each found a way to adapt.

Marjorie—who had received provisional authorization to vote her husband's shares—insisted on a more active role at the newspaper.

Jay acted immediately to appease his mother. He offered a motion for Marjorie to replace her husband as board president, and included a provision elevating him from managing editor to acting CEO. Although reactions among his siblings were mixed, the proposal eventually won approval.

Declining revenues, however, rattled solidarity. Jay blamed the downturn in readership and advertising revenue on competition from 24-hour news sources and digital information providers. He contended mail-order giants were crushing brick-and-mortar retailers, eliminating or downsizing advertising budgets.

Jay proposed moving forward with building a state-of-the-art printing plant—an idea that had been put on hold after the patriarch's disappearance. He argued a new press would attract outside print jobs to offset losses and fulfill his father's desire to preserve the print edition.

His reasoning, however, failed to win support from other family members, who equivocated or balked at the massive costs of the project.

What became apparent to all was that the bonds that united family did not necessarily translate into harmony among board members. The consensus was Jay was competent, but did not share his father's leadership qualities.

In appearance, Jay looked much like his father—someone a casting director might consider for a swashbuckler role. He was tall—nearly 6-feet, 2-inches—with an athletic bearing and a hint of swagger in his gait. His sandy blond hair was longish and swept back, and his mustache was neatly trimmed.

What Jay lacked was an appearance of sincerity—a quality his father personified.

Amid the discord about the newspaper's future, Henry, then Anne, resigned their positions to accept job offers elsewhere, although they remained shareholders and retained membership on the newspaper board.

The business fragmentation resulted in family tension, evidenced by the silence that prevailed at the dining table as the sound of clinking cutlery diminished.

When Anne stood and began clearing the table, Jay said to George, "So, little brother, how goes Grindell's campaign for sheriff?"

"Good," George replied, "but it would be a whole lot better with an editorial endorsement from the paper. I wish you'd reconsider."

"You know we don't do endorsements anymore," Jay said. He lifted his napkin and wiped his mustache and mouth.

"I know that was Dad's decision," George said, "But that doesn't mean we can't restart it."

"Father stopped it for a good reason," Anne said. "He felt if you endorsed one candidate, it just created ill will among supporters of the opponent."

"You mean advertisers," George countered. "Dad didn't want to create ill will among advertisers. You and Henry were the ones who put that bug in Dad's ear when you were the chief bean counter, Anne. But you're not anymore, so butt out. I say if we're going to have any editorial influence, we need to take a stand—on issues and on candidates."

"We'll take a look at it," Jay said, "but for future election cycles, not this one."

"I'm not asking you to consider the entire slate of candidates," George said. "Just Grindell."

"And how would that look?" Jay asked.

"Like we really believe Grindell is the best choice for Huhman County."

"I think it would look like we're desperate to get him

elected," Jay said. "And what if he loses? It would make us losers. It's bad enough that I let you talk me into becoming one of his biggest contributors. It's already common knowledge that you and I are backing him financially. And, if it isn't, it will be when we publish the campaign finance reports."

"We don't have to publish them," George said.

"We always have," Jay said. "I'm not breaking with tradition and risking the newspaper's integrity just to indulge your personal resentments."

"It's hardly a personal resentment," George protested, his anger rising. "Hood botched the investigation of Dad's disappearance. It's unforgivable. He needs to be replaced and we should all be together in this."

"I'm with you," Jay said, his tone calming, "but we need to be deliberate. We can't go off half-cocked and do more harm than good, particularly for the newspaper."

Although George seemed somewhat mollified, he remained sullenly silent as Anne continued clearing the table.

"How's Chip working out?" Jay finally asked his brother, referencing Grindell's campaign manager.

"Pretty well, I guess." George replied.

"You guess?" Jay stroked his mustache. "For what we're paying him, he needs to do better than pretty well. He's supposed to be the best election demographer in Missouri."

"I don't know," Anne said, as she lifted Jay's empty plate. "I know Chip Luther has managed some successful statewide campaigns, and I'm sure demographics are valuable at the statewide level, but—"

"Valuable?" Jay cut in. "They're essential."

"All I'm saying is in a county election, I would think campaigning door-to-door, getting to know the voters, would be top priority."

"And you'd be wrong," Jay countered. "We hired Chip so Steve Grindell wouldn't be wasting time glad-handing rubes at grocery stores and kissing babies in shopping carts. Stick to your social work, sister. No need to advise when you don't know what you're talking about."

"Children," Marjorie scolded. "Be respectful."

Although Anne had tried to enure herself to her brother's patrician attitude, she was rankled. She glared at Jay and he responded in kind, creating a silent stalemate interrupted by the ringing of the doorbell.

Anne dropped the dirty plate back in front of Jay. "I'll get it," she said, her tone brusque.

As she left the dining room, Jay glanced through the window and saw the sheriff's cruiser. "Speaking of chief rube," he whispered, loud enough for those around the table to hear.

Anne opened the front door and greeted the sheriff.

"I noticed the cars out front," Hood said, "and remembered your weekly dinner. I hope I'm not disturbing—"

"No, no" Anne said. "We're finished. I was just clearing the table."

She led Hood to the dining room, where he was met with expressions ranging from Marjorie's anticipation to Jay's surprise to George's disdain.

Hood focused on Marjorie. "My apologies," he said. He

held his hat by his fingertips.

"You remember my brothers," Anne said, pointing to each as she added, "Jay and George."

"Of course," Hood said, a half-truth. He recognized Jay immediately. With the exception of maturity and a mustache, he looked much the same as Hood remembered him.

George, however, had changed noticeably since he captained the defensive line and led the football team in quarterback sacks. George's former coach, Hood thought, would be dismayed at the toll time and indolence had taken on the man's appearance and physique. George's hair had thinned and grayed, his taut facial features and muscles had slackened, and his abdomen had become paunchy.

As the sheriff approached, Jay stood and accepted his handshake.

Hood continued around the table toward George, who retained a smug smirk and remained seated with his hands folded. When Hood realized George had no intention to shake hands, he bypassed the youngest brother and stood beside Anne.

"The reason I'm here," Hood said, addressing Marjorie, "is I wanted to let you know that, based on a preliminary examination, the arm found in the woods almost certainly belongs to your husband."

Marjorie lowered her head and stared at the tabletop.

"*Almost* certainly?" Jay asked.

"The medical records match, including evidence of a healed fracture of the upper arm bone—humerus, I think Loeffelman called it."

"Anne said the arm was found near Cooper Creek, by the Trestle," Jay said.

"That's correct. We've initiated a search, but so far—"

"That's miles from the site where he said he was going," Jay interrupted.

"I'm aware of that, but because we found the arm, we need to search the area for—"

"For his body, I presume?" George asked.

"And for possible evidence. Loss of an arm is—" Hood stopped, recalling his conversation with the medical examiner and searching for the right word, "well, it's significant, but it doesn't necessarily mean your father is deceased."

George snorted a derisive laugh. "Come on, Sheriff," he said. "We're all grown-ups here. Are you implying my father is still alive?"

"George," Marjorie scolded.

"We're exploring all possibilities," Hood said.

"Now," George said, "you sound more like a politician than a sheriff."

"I'm sorry." Hood looked at his fingertips slowly twirling his hat by the brim.

"That's it?" George's question was fraught with finality and frustration.

"I'm sorry about the news. I'm sorry I interrupted your family gathering. I'd better get back."

"I'll see you out," Anne said, eager to end his discomfort. She frowned at her brothers as she escorted Hood to the door.

CHAPTER 5

Dawn awakened slowly, casting faint light on a gray landscape as Hood steered his cruiser onto the shoulder of Schoolhouse Road.

He exited and approached his rookie deputy, Young John, who leaned against his vehicle, which he had parked strategically to block media members and curiosity seekers from the gravel road leading to the search scene. Young John had acquired the moniker not because he was young—although, at age 22, he was—but to distinguish him from an older deputy named John.

"Morning," Hood greeted as he approached. "Any news?"

"Nothing yet," Young John said. "But they're already gathering to start at first light." He gestured to the roadside where the outline of a mid-sized sedan was barely visible in the morning haze. "And at least one reporter isn't giving up either."

"Wadkins?" Hood speculated.

Young John nodded.

"Has he been here all night?"

"Uh huh. I think he finally fell asleep in his car."

"What'd you tell him?"

"Just what we agreed to put in the press release—time, date, place, facts. I handed a copy to every reporter who showed up. The others all left when they realized that was all the information they were going to get for the time being."

"I'll go talk to him. He deserves some face time, at least."

Hood walked to the vehicle and assessed the newspapers, clippings, file folders, and official documents piled to the windows in the passenger and rear seats. Robert Wadkins sat in the driver's seat, his head cradled by the headrest as he snored gently.

Hood tapped on the window, which was partially open.

Wadkins startled awake. "Sheriff," he said, mildly surprised.

"Sleeping it off?" Hood asked. He tended to tease Wadkins because he genuinely liked the guy. Wadkins was one of the few remaining "old school" journalists. He covered his beat—crime and the courts—like a blanket. He insisted on accuracy and, to that end, he recorded every news conference, interview, and conversation. And Hood knew from experience that if Wadkins agreed to hear something "off the record," the sheriff wouldn't need to worry about reading it in a news story.

Wadkins got out of his car. He wore a rumpled pin-striped suit jacket with casual slacks. Missing was his customary necktie, which often depicted some novelty character or motif. As always, Hood thought Wadkins could benefit greatly from proper nutrition, exercise, and grooming. And, as always, Hood reminded himself that was none of his business; he was not a lifestyle coach. "I'm in the market for more information," Wadkins said. "I filed a story based on what little was in your news release—should be in the morning edition—but, you know, today's a new day."

"I just got here," Hood replied, his tone sincere. "Right now, you know as much as I do. If I find out anything new, I'll update you before I leave. Fair enough?"

"Fair enough."

Moments later, Hood parked in the clearing at the Trestle site. He grabbed the container of coffee he had brought and walked to a makeshift command post—two lawn chairs and a card table shaded by a retractable stand-alone awning. Nearby was a tarp strewn with empty beer and soda cans; liquor bottles; fast-food cups, wrappers, and containers; an old ball cap; a pair of mismatched socks; a pair of panties; and other trash.

Wally sat in one of the chairs, speaking on a radio and marking a map spread on the table.

"Coffee?" Hood asked when the radio conversation ended.

Wally nodded and Hood poured.

"Find anything?" Hood asked. He handed the cup to his chief deputy.

Wally pointed to the tarp. "Just junk so far. Searchers are getting in position. We're hoping for better luck today."

"We may need to expand the search area. Loeffelman thinks an animal could have carried the arm a ways."

"It'll take time. Sun's just coming up and it looks like we're in for another scorcher. Yesterday was slow going, exhausting. I need to make sure these guys take time to rest, cool off, get rehydrated."

"Of course. Loeffelman also reminded me to have them pay particular attention to areas that seem more lush than their surroundings."

"The decomposition thing."

"Exactly," Hood said. "What quadrant are we concentrating on now?"

"Southeast." Wally pointed to an area on the map. "We've covered the northwest quadrant where the arm was found. This morning, we moved—" Wally added, halting in mid-sentence when Hood's cell phone rang.

Hood looked at the screen, indicating the caller was Young John. "What's up, John," he answered.

"Got a lady here who says she needs to talk to you. Name's Anne Bishop."

"Let her through." Hood ended the call, turned to Wally and said, "Anne Bishop wants to talk to me."

"What about?"

"No idea. You said the northwest quadrant is clear?"

Wally nodded as they watched a silver BMW approach, a trail of gravel dust in its wake. Anne parked beside Hood's cruiser, emerged from the driver's seat, and approached.

"Sheriff," she greeted. "Deputy Wallendorf, if I remember correctly."

Hood recalled the two had met because it was Wally who had interviewed Anne following her stepfather's disappearance.

"Correct, Miss Bishop," Wally said.

"Please call me Anne."

Wally nodded.

Anne turned to the sheriff. "I was wondering if I might have a word with you?"

"Of course," Hood said.

"In private," she added.

Hood was baffled. He wondered if he had overlooked something when he spoke with the family or if she had additional questions. He looked to the northwest quadrant, where a trail paralleled the riverbank and the Trestle loomed overhead. "Let's take a walk."

"Have you found anything yet?" Anne asked.

"Just what's there." He gestured to the items on the tarp. "It will all be tagged and bagged to be analyzed, but I'm not expecting it will tell us anything."

"I'm learning that," Anne said.

"What's that?"

"To keep my expectations low." They stopped within the ribbon of shade afforded by the Trestle. "After my father disappeared, I expected every phone call to be from him or from someone with an answer, an explanation. Now—" she shrugged, leaving the sentence incomplete.

Hood thought about how her words matched one of the concepts in his program of recovery. He had been advised to avoid expectations, which—if not attained—might result in disappointments and resentments.

"During high school," Anne said, gazing at the Trestle's undergirding, "did you ever bring girls out here?"

"Not much." Hood realized he sounded evasive, so he added, "You ever come out here?"

"Greg Henderson brought me here once," she said.

Hood noticed her vacant look as she focused on the memory.

"It was Friday night, April 12, 1991," Anne recalled. "Greg took me to Millie's Diner and I had a cheeseburger, fries, and a chocolate shake. Then he asked if I wanted to take a walk along the creek. It was a nice evening and I was having a good time, so I said 'sure.' We stopped at one point—right about here—and he leaned in to kiss me and it was nice. Then he got all handsy and started this awkward groping that just seemed comically absurd. In a split second the mood went from romantic to pathetic."

Hood shook his head, signaling disbelief. "I have no idea how you can recall all that."

"It's more than recall," she said, as they began walking leisurely along the trail. "I mean, I see the entire episode like I'm watching a video, but I also experience the feelings, emotions, sensations. It's more than remembering, it's reliving."

"I'm not sure I'd like that," Hood said.

"It can be a blessing or a curse. People say it's a gift and, in some situations, it is," Anne said. "But not always. One thing I've learned is people don't like being corrected when they share a memory. My ex-husband was a case in point it. Whenever he told a story about something that happened to us, I'd jump in and correct him. It wasn't even a conscious thing. I guess I'm just a stickler for accuracy. Anyway, it caused a rift in our marriage, but it was just one of many. In retrospect, I don't think we were meant to be together."

Anne plucked a bunch of blue flowers from beside the trail, wistfully detached a blossom and cast it into the breeze. "I did learn a lesson, though. I'm less apt to correct people when they're wrong. If it's not important," she added, as she tossed another flower, "I just let it go."

Hood was reminded of how his own attitudes and behaviors had changed during his time in recovery.

"But some things," Anne continued, "I can't change."

Hood felt a shiver, as if she were commenting on his thoughts.

"I can't control when a memory is triggered," she said. "It can be very intrusive, particularly when they come one after another. When it happens—and it happens a lot—I'm right back there. It makes it hard to live in the moment."

Hood was reminded again about his program of recovery and the advice to stay in the present, which seemed difficult enough without a domineering memory.

"What's worse," Anne continued, "is there are some things I'd like to forget, but can't." She removed another flower and released it.

"Such as?"

"Such as what really happened the morning my father disappeared."

Hood stopped abruptly and faced her. "What do you mean?"

"Mother and I talked it over and decided it was time you knew the truth."

The word galvanized his attention. "The truth?" he repeated.

"Our family's collective alibi was a lie. We were not together at the house when my father disappeared. He left the house much earlier. Mother thinks it might have been as early as 7:30 that morning, hours before Jay, George, or I arrived."

Confusion, disbelief, and anger collided in Hood's mind. "All of you were eliminated as suspects back then because you shared an alibi," Hood said. "What you just told me changes everything."

"I know," Anne said. She dropped the remaining flowers and hung her head penitently.

"Whose idea was it to create this collective alibi?"

"Mother's," Anne said. "But it doesn't matter. We all agreed to it."

"You know I'll need to reinterview each of you." Hood exhaled a protracted sigh. "All this time that's passed," he said, almost to himself. "Evidence disappears, witnesses die or move away, memories fade—"

"Mine don't," she reminded him.

"I'll get it," Hood said, responding to the doorbell chime.

"Thanks, hon." Linda stood at the stove, busily stirring her homemade brown gravy.

Hood paused and inhaled a deep breath to gather himself before opening the front door to their guests, Otto and Sarah Kampeter. Hood wasn't sure if he harbored a resentment against Sarah, but he knew he had become uncomfortable around her. Although his recovery program asked him to listen and learn from the experience of other alcoholics—Sarah had been sober more than a decade—Hood often felt she was judging him. She seemed to mean well, but Hood couldn't shake the feeling she was scrutinizing the quality of his sobriety. He felt much more at ease around Otto, who was among the most transparent and unpretentious people he ever had encountered.

Hood pulled open the door and began an exchange of greetings that continued as they proceeded to the kitchen.

Sarah held a square, white box by the white string tied around it. When she asked them to guess, both Francis and Linda correctly speculated it was a pie from Millie's Diner, but failed to identify it as blueberry.

Drinks were offered—water and iced tea were selected—and Sarah joined her sister bringing bowls of food to the table while Hood and Otto talked about the campaign.

"So," Otto said, "how many yard signs did you put out the other day?"

"One."

"Very funny."

"I'm not kidding," Hood said. "I got called away. Elizabeth and her friend found an arm bone in the woods by the Trestle."

"Sarah said Linda called her about that and then I saw the story in the local paper. They haven't confirmed whose arm it is, but—"

"I really can't say anything about it."

"I understand," Otto said. "I'm not asking you to. I'm just saying if the arm belongs to old man Bishop, it could create some complications with the campaign."

"How so?"

"George hired Chip Luther to manage your opponent's

campaign. Chip's a pro; he'll use the discovery of the arm to remind people the case—your case—remains unsolved after all these months. With the Bishops bankrolling the campaign, I don't need to tell you—"

"I know," Hood repeated, a tinge of frustration in his tone.

"I know how you feel about campaigning. I get it. Politics, fundraising, re-election—it's a pain. All I'm saying—"

"Dinner's ready," Linda called.

Hood felt momentary relief as everyone made their way to the table, passed serving bowls, and filled their plates.

As soon as the activity waned, Sarah focused on Hood and asked, "So, have you identified whose arm it was?"

"That information hasn't been released yet."

"My money's on James Bishop," Sarah said. "I always thought there was something, you know, not accidental about that whole thing." When no one replied, she laid her fork beside her plate and added, "How's Elizabeth taking all this? Is she okay?"

"She's fine," Linda answered.

"Is she here?" Sarah asked. "I'd like to talk—"

"She's at her friend, Claire's," Hood said. He heard curtness in his voice, and immediately regretted it.

"That's how I used to avoid boring dinners with my parents and their relatives," Otto said. "I'd say I've been invited to dinner at a friend's house."

"Fine. Fine. I'll change the subject," Sarah said. "Francis, how's your recovery program?"

Otto and Sarah were among the few family members

who knew he was a recovering alcoholic. Hood's wife and daughter knew, of course, as did his older sister, who lived and worked in Maryland. His parents were deceased.

The members of the recovery group hosted by Matthew, Hood's sponsor, also knew, but they observed the tradition of confidentiality. And he had confided in two of his co-workers—Wally and Maggie. Young John may have guessed his boss had firsthand knowledge of alcoholism, if only because Hood had helped connect Young John to recovery resources.

"Pretty good, I think," Hood answered. "I still think about drinking sometimes, but that daily obsession is gone."

"I think he's doing great," Linda added. "I can see the changes."

"Often," Sarah said, "the people around the alcoholic are the first to notice the changes." She turned to Otto. "Was that true for you, dear?"

"Absolutely," Otto affirmed.

"I don't know how he put up with me," Sarah said. "I was a mean, miserable drunk."

"Francis mostly kept to himself," Linda said, "but you know all that."

"I'd just sit in my recliner, switch on the TV, and drink until I blacked out or passed out," Hood said. "I didn't talk about it much, but I do remember getting pretty defensive whenever Linda said something about my drinking."

"That's common," Sarah said.

"At first, I stopped pointing it out," Linda said, "just to keep the peace. But, after I while, I couldn't help myself. I know

I became a nag."

"And I responded by trying to hide my drinking," Hood said.

"That's typically how it works," Sarah said.

"Well." Otto lifted his glass filled with iced tea. "I propose we change the subject again—from troubles of yesterday to the good company we're enjoying right now."

"Hear, hear," they said, and clinked glasses.

CHAPTER 6

"We found it!"

Hood heard Wally's words emanate from the phone before he had even brought it to his ear. He knew immediately what "it" was. "Where?" he asked.

"More than a mile from the Trestle. It's a densely wooded area."

"Any identification? Wallet?"

"We haven't touched it."

"Have you called forensics or the M.E.?"

"No. You were my first call."

"Okay," Hood said. "I'm on my way. I'll round up Loeffelman and someone from the crime lab. Stay there and preserve the scene."

"Will do," Wally said. "By the way, there's an easier way to get here. Continue on Schoolhouse Road past the turnoff to the Trestle. The road winds around, but just before the woods give way to a clearing, there's an access road with a gate. Go ahead and park there. We've got a four-wheeler here, so I'll send somebody to meet you."

"Great."

Minutes later, Hood was driving his cruiser to the scene, accompanied by Loeffelman and Sandra Brondel, a forensic analyst from the Missouri Highway Patrol crime lab. Although he wasn't superstitious by nature, Hood was enjoying what he considered a rare lucky streak. The body had been found, trudging through the woods wouldn't be necessary, and both Loeffelman and Sandra were immediately available.

Hood had worked with Sandra on previous cases and he routinely asked for her by name when he needed the services of the crime lab. She was without artifice—personally and professionally. She used minimal makeup and gathered her long, tawny hair into a simple ponytail, creating an impression that was simultaneously natural and breathtaking.

As promised, the trio was met by a searcher Hood recognized as Phil Graessle, a member of the Sheriff's Patrol, a group of trained volunteers who assisted with searches, security at county events, and other behind-the-scenes duties.

After Phil greeted the sheriff and introduced himself to the others, they climbed aboard an all-terrain vehicle, which Phil steered around a padlocked gate—designed to restrict entry by full-sized vehicles—and along a partially overgrown trail. Hood guessed it had been cleared for hunting or logging, but was not used frequently. They were bounced and jostled as the ATV crossed a dry creek bed, crested a ridge, and arrived at the site.

Wally greeted them as they disembarked and pointed to an area more overgrown and verdant than its surroundings. From Hood's vantage point, the remains appeared to be something between a partially connected skeleton and a jumbled pile of random bones. He observed remnants of a pale blue windbreaker, white polo shirt, khaki slacks, walking shoes, and rubber boots consistent with the clothing James Bishop reportedly was wearing when he disappeared.

To avoid further contaminating the scene or interfering with the work of the medical examiner and forensic analyst, Hood directed them to get started while he lingered with Wally and Phil near the ATV.

"You find him or one of the team?" Hood asked his chief deputy.

"Phil did," Wally said.

"By the way," Phil added, "that tip about the lush surroundings really helped. That's what first caught my attention."

"Did you have to disturb the site much to, you know, get a better look?" Hood asked.

"I stepped in fairly close and moved some of that tall grass, but as soon as I saw the bones, I backed off and called Wally."

"Good," Hood said.

"I'm going to get me some water," Phil said. "You guys want anything?"

When they declined, Phil joined the group of searchers who were gathered in the shade of a large cottonwood tree.

As the sheriff and his chief deputy stood together in silence, a barely audible, intermittent noise registered with Hood.

"You hearing what I'm hearing?" Hood asked.

"It's traffic noise from Schoolhouse Road," Wally said.

"Exactly," Hood said, "Since the arm bone was found the other day, I've been assuming the Trestle lot was the starting point, but now I'm thinking that trail we just used would provide easier access."

"Let's have a look," Wally said.

Hood alerted Loeffelman and Sandra of their plan to borrow the ATV, which they used to retrace the route. When they arrived at the gate where the trail intersected Schoolhouse Road, Hood said, "Drive down the road a ways. I want to see what's around here."

"It's illegal to drive a four-wheeler on a county road," Wally said. He tried not to smile, but failed.

"Don't worry," Hood said. "I'll be your character witness."

They traveled north on Schoolhouse Road through wooded areas on both sides until reaching the intersection with Route TT, then reversed and drove south. Less than a mile beyond the intersection with the gated trail, the woods ended, yielding to a large clearing posted with signs that read: For Sale, Call 573-635-3316 for information.

"Stop here a minute," Hood said.

Wally pulled to the roadside and stopped.

"Do you know who owns this land?" Hood asked.

"No idea," Wally said. "It'll be in the plat books at the recorder's office."

Hood took a notepad from his pocket and copied the telephone number. "You think Bishop might have been looking at this site for the printing plant?"

Wally shrugged. "Seems kind of out of the way. If they bring in newsprint by the truckload, you'd think they'd at least want a site on a highway."

"You'd think," Hood agreed. "Maybe even a rail spur." He tucked the notepad into a pocket. "Okay, we better head back."

They returned to the scene, which looked much the same as when they had left. Loeffelman and Sandra seemed to move around each other in some choreographed dance as each examined the remains and scrutinized the surroundings.

After what seemed a long time but probably wasn't, Loeffelman looked up at the sheriff and said, "Francis, look here."

Hood stepped closer and, as directed by the medical examiner, focused on a hole in the skull.

"I'll need to do a more thorough examination," Loeffelman said, his tone somber, "but it appears this man was shot in the head."

"Let's begin," Matthew said, "with the Serenity Prayer, followed by a moment of silence for those still suffering from their addictions."

Hood joined about a dozen voices reciting the familiar prayer. Although he bowed his head slightly during the ensuing silence, he glanced at the diverse group of men and women seated with him in metal chairs at a rectangular arrangement of folding tables.

The venue was the basement of St. Cecilia Catholic Church, which served a variety of sacred and secular functions, including gymnasium, nursery, Sunday School classroom, wedding reception site, meeting place for community groups, and, on occasion, polling place.

On Thursday evenings, it was the gathering place for Recovery Rules, a weekly meeting hosted by Matthew, Hood's sponsor. Although most of the participants were alcoholics, people suffering from any addiction—drugs, gambling, eating disorders—were welcome.

"To begin," Matthew said, ending the shared silence, "does anyone have anything to report, any issues on your heart or mind?"

When no one spoke, Matthew continued, "Okay, what I thought we'd discuss this evening is honesty. I believe honesty is at the core of recovery because if I can't be honest with myself, I'll continue to wallow in justification, rationalization, and denial."

Hood thought immediately of his conversation with Anne at the Trestle. If she—or any of the family members, for that matter—had been honest with him from the start, he wouldn't be revisiting an inactive case and might have had a better chance to solve the disappearance and provide closure for the Bishops.

"So," Matthew continued, "honesty is the topic. Who wants to start?"

"Hi, my name's Mac and I'm an alcoholic."

Hood joined the greeting and focused on the man who had more time in recovery than Matthew and always shared insights Hood found useful.

"You said it when you introduced the topic, Matthew," Mac said. "For me, the toughest thing—tougher than getting honest with others—was getting honest with myself. I justified my drinking by telling myself I deserved it because I worked hard to support my family. I also hid behind a shield of denial, telling myself I wasn't hurting anybody else. What a crock. I was an absentee husband and father. I was physically in the room, but I wasn't there mentally, emotionally, or spiritually. I was selfish and I had to be dishonest to be okay with that. When my drinking got worse and I couldn't believe my own lies anymore, the self-loathing really kicked in. I couldn't look at myself in the mirror. By the grace of my higher power, I got into recovery. I finally began to see how dishonest I had been with myself. That's all."

Mac's words prompted Hood to think about the topic and, as the sharing continued, he found himself contemplating instead of listening. He admitted his drinking was coupled with deceit, but had he embraced honesty in sobriety? Was honesty an either-or proposition, or were there shades of gray? He knew better than to say something mean if he didn't like someone's outfit or hair style, but did he expand that to other situations to avoid being honest? He thought about his relationship with his wife and daughter. He was so happy to have them back that he sometimes felt he was walking on eggshells around them. And he knew his caution was based on fear—fear that he would say or do something that would alienate them, if not physically, at least emotionally.

When the sharing eventually moved to Hood, he introduced himself and added, "I'm just going to listen and learn tonight. I'll pass."

CHAPTER 7

Hood was delighted. He had scanned the morning newspaper and scrolled through social media posts, but found no mention of a body being found.

Although he had urged everyone involved in the discovery to withhold the information until the remains were identified and next of kin were notified, he hadn't expected compliance, particularly since Wadkins—who seemed to have sources everywhere—was sniffing around the investigation.

Hood flipped through his notebook, found the phone number for the real estate company, and called.

"Rackers Real Estate Professionals. This is Alicia, how may I direct your call?"

"Good morning, Alicia. This is your sheriff, Francis Hood. I copied this number from a land-for-sale sign on Schoolhouse Road.

"Yes. Jerry Rackers is handling that property. I'll connect you."

Hood awaited the transfer, followed almost immediately by the greeting, "This is Jerry. What can I do for you?"

Hood introduced himself, identified the tract of land that was the basis of his call, and asked, "How long have you had that property listed?"

"Are you interested?" Jerry asked, his tone brightening.

"No," Hood said. "Just seeking information."

"Well, I hate to say it, but it's been over a year now."

"Did a James Bishop ever contact you about that property?"

"No," Jerry said, without hesitation.

"You seem certain. He publishes the local newspaper. At least, he did before he disappeared in August."

"Sheriff, I've only received two inquiries about that property in all the time I've been trying to sell it. Commercial clients aren't interested because the only access is a winding, two-lane road. A residential development would be ideal, except there's no zoning in the county so there's no guarantee a rendering plant or salvage yard won't move in next door."

"Can you tell me the names of the other two people who inquired?"

"I'm obligated to keep that confidential."

Hood wondered whether confidentiality was a law or an industry standard, and whether a court order would be worth pursuing. "Can you at least tell me if you were contacted by any members of the Bishop family?"

"I suppose I can tell you who didn't inquire. None was a Bishop and—as far as I know—none was acting on their behalf."

"Thanks," Hood said.

After they disconnected, he resumed his morning routine, reading incident reports from the overnight shift.

He was reading the narrative of a theft from a vehicle when his phone rang. The screen identified the caller as Loeffelman. Hood answered.

"Your autopsy's done," Loeffelman said.

"That was quick."

"Not much to examine. A partial skeleton with some assembly required offers more questions than answers."

"Is it James Bishop?"

"That I can answer. Yes," Loeffelman said. "When can you come by?"

"On my way." Hood disconnected, advised Maggie of his destination, and crossed the drive separating the courthouse from the annex.

The two county officials exchanged greetings, and Hood followed Loeffelman to a long table where bones, including unconnected ones, were arranged in the image of an incomplete skeleton. On display on a nearby cart were personal items—a wallet and its contents, keys, comb, etc.—and what remained of the clothing and accessories. Hood recalled Marjorie's mention of rubber overshoes. He had assumed they were the form-fitting, ankle-high shoe coverings, but noted these were the shin-high, four-buckle variety.

"We found James Bishop's laminated driver's license in the wallet," the medical examiner said. "More important, dental records match and the arm matches. The evidence establishes these are the remains of James Bishop. The downside is he isn't revealing many secrets regarding what happened."

"At the scene, you said he'd been shot."

"I believe I said he appears to have been shot. The skull has entry and exit holes consistent with being penetrated by a bullet of sufficient force and velocity to enter the front and exit the back. The trajectory indicates a slightly downward angle from front to back, but the precise angle can't be determined because we don't know where the gunshot originated. And," Loeffelman added, with emphasis, "we have no bullet."

"Any idea how long he's been dead?"

"Hard to make a determination. What we've got here is skeletonization—a later phase in the breakdown of a body after death. Skeletonization can occur anywhere from four months to more than a decade, depending on a range of variables. These bones are like bringing a musician a violin without strings. He can identify the instrument, but can't play a concerto."

"But if Bishop's death coincided with his disappearance in August, that would be—" Hood paused momentarily to do the math, "nearly eleven months."

Loeffelman shrugged. "Remember, Francis, I deal in facts. Exploring possibilities based on those facts is your job."

"But," Hood said, "if he were in the woods with your variables—snow, freezing, thawing, coyotes, vultures, insects—eleven months would be reasonable."

"Not unreasonable," Loeffelman said.

"Any new evidence to suggest how the arm got detached?" Hood asked.

"There are no striations indicating use of a saw, knife, or other type of blade." Loeffelman retrieved a thin manila folder and handed it to Hood. "This is your copy of the autopsy. It's short on facts, but it teems with possibilities for you to explore."

* * * * *

As Hood approached the circular drive in front of the Bishop's Tudor home, he spotted a row of high-end vehicles, including Anne's BMW, a Range Rover, and a Corvette convertible. Parked separately, as if poised for a getaway, was a pickup truck that appeared to be a work in progress. Its color was faded red and it was outfitted with a dingy white camper shell. The passenger door was dented, but the hood and both fenders were unmarred and primed, indicating they had been reshaped or replaced.

After his visit with Loeffelman, Hood had called Anne and asked her to try to gather her mother, brothers Jay and George, and former foster brother Julian at 2 p.m. at Marjorie's house. He explained his intention was to brief them simultaneously on recent findings.

Hood parked and exited his cruiser. As he studied the vehicles, he considered the possibility that one of them might have been used to transport the family patriarch's body. He removed his pocket pad, noted the license number and description of each vehicle, then wrote: Were these the vehicles the children owned when James disappeared?

As he returned the pad and pen to his pocket, Anne hailed him from atop the stone steps.

Hood ascended and, when they met, Anne placed her hands on his shoulders and kissed him lightly on the cheek. He was flummoxed by the unexpected greeting, which struck him as simultaneously casual and somehow intimate.

"Thanks for coming." She stepped back.

"Thanks for setting this up." He intentionally slowed his breathing in an attempt to regain his composure. "I appreciate it."

"Come in," Anne invited. "They're all here except Henry, of course, but I've got him on speaker phone."

As Hood followed Anne into the expansive family room, he focused immediately on Julian, who looked entirely out of place among the well-groomed, well-dressed family members who occupied the ornate furnishings. Julian's gaunt facial features were framed by longer, wilder hair and a patchy, scruffy beard. He wore stained jeans and a faded T-shirt.

"You remember Julian?" Anne said.

"Of course," Hood said. He approached Julian, who arose from his chair and accepted a handshake.

Also seated separately in chairs were Marjorie and George. Jay and a woman Hood hadn't met were seated beside each other on a sofa.

"And this is Jay's wife, Diane," Anne said.

After they greeted each other, Anne continued, "Please, have a seat, Sheriff." She faced the phone. "Henry, can you hear us?"

"Yes," Henry's disembodied voice replied.

"Good," she said. "The sheriff asked if we could gather so he could provide an update on Father and answer any questions we may have." She faced Hood.

"Thanks for being here," Hood said. He shifted in his chair, bent forward, and fidgeted with his hat, which he held by its brim. "I wish I was here under different circumstances, but it's better if you all hear the same thing at the same time. I'm sorry to have to tell you that we found additional human remains in the woods and the body has been identified as James Bishop."

Marjorie stared at him, her expression unchanged. Anne sighed a low moan. George shook his head in "I-told-you-so" fashion, but, otherwise, the brothers remained silent, as if any display of emotion would eliminate them from some unnamed macho competition.

"The discovery," Hood said, "was made about a mile from the Trestle site where the arm was found earlier."

"You found my husband?" Marjorie asked. Her voice was faint, wounded.

Anne intercepted the question. "The sheriff found his remains, Mother. He's gone."

"Where is he?" Marjorie persisted.

"I think she wants to know where the remains are," Jay said.

"At the medical examiner's," Hood answered, "but if you know what funeral home you want to use, we can make arrangements for the transfer."

As he spoke, Marjorie arose and left the room.

"We use Fredrickson's Mortuary," Anne said. "Excuse me, I'd better go check on Mother." She stood and followed.

"How long's he been dead?" George asked. His tone was emotionless, as if asking for the time.

"The medical examiner said it's been some time. It's possible he died the day he disappeared."

"How'd the body get from the development site to the Trestle area?" George asked. "It's clear across the county."

"We don't know," Hood said. "There is a tract of land

for sale on Schoolhouse Road not far from where we found the remains. Do any of you know if he might have been considering that as a site for the proposed printing plant?"

Jay shook his head. "Schoolhouse Road is too narrow to provide sufficient access."

The observation, Hood thought, was consistent with what he had been told by the real estate agent. "Did any of you contact Rackers Real Estate Professionals or Jerry Rackers, who is handling the sale?"

They exchanged looks, creating a protracted silence until Jay said, "I know I didn't."

"Me neither," George said. "I have no clue how my father ended up out there."

"But we found his car at the site out east—where he said he was going," Jay said.

"Maybe somebody picked him up there and drove him to the Schoolhouse Road area," Julian speculated.

"Or somebody killed him at the eastern site and moved his body," George said.

"We're exploring all—" Hood began.

"All possibilities," George interrupted. "Yeah, we know that."

"How'd he die?" Henry's voice asked from the telephone speaker.

"Based on the medical examiner's findings," Hood began, choosing his words carefully, "the most likely explanation is he suffered a bullet wound to the head."

"It can't be," Marjorie said.

Everyone focused on the matriarch, who had returned to the room and stood beside Anne near the doorway.

"Who would kill Father?" Anne asked.

"He had enemies," George replied.

"Not everyone shared his political views," Anne said, "but that's just the nature of the business. I wouldn't exactly call them enemies."

"Did you recover a bullet?" Henry asked, effectively ending the disagreement between Anne and George.

"No," Hood said.

"Was he shot from up close or far away?" George asked.

"No determination could be made."

"Head shots are tricky, especially from far away," Julian said. "It would take one hell of a marksman to kill someone from any distance with a single shot."

"Julian," Marjorie scolded.

"Really, Julian," Anne echoed.

Julian raised his arms and spread his hands slightly in a sign of mock surrender. "I'm just asking what we're all wondering. Everybody knows we've got some good shooters in this family."

His observation was not lost on Hood, who was aware of the competitive marksmen titles Marjorie had amassed in her younger years. He also knew she had taught shooting skills to her children, with varying results.

"We just want to know," Jay said, as if apologizing for Julian's crude choice of words, "how our father died and who killed him. That's all."

"So do I," Hood responded before anyone else could join the conversation. "You have every right to ask questions. We're not at cross-purposes here. We all want answers, but a lot of time has passed, there's a lot we don't know, and what little we do know leads to a lot of possibilities. I'll need to interview each of you again. I'd like—"

"You mean now that we're all suspects," George said.

"What I'd like," Hood said, ignoring the interruption, "is for each of you to write down where you were and what you were doing on the Saturday and the Sunday morning before James disappeared. And if you were with him in the days leading up to that, did you notice any changes in him? Did he seem nervous, worried, anything?"

"That was almost a year ago," George said.

"I understand, but I'm asking you to bear with me. In my experience, I've learned when people write things down it can trigger memories they didn't even know they had."

"Me, too?" Diane asked.

"Yes."

"But I wasn't here that day," she said, a mild protest. "I didn't come to dinner."

"I wasn't here, either," Julian said. "I was in Iowa. Remember?"

"Please," Hood said. "I'm only asking you to write what you remember."

"Just have Annie do it and save us the trouble," Jay said. "She's the one with the freak memory."

"Children." Marjorie's shriek was louder than Hood thought

possible. "Enough. Stop bickering." She glared, in turn, at each child, signaling she would suffer no further discussion or dissension, then said. "We'll all cooperate. Won't we?"

Hood observed the collective nods and bobbing of heads. "Thank you," he said. "I'll be making arrangements to visit with each of you individually—at your convenience, of course, but soon."

"Is there anything else we can do for you?" Anne asked.

"I don't think so," Hood answered. "Of course," he added, as she stood, "I'll keep you updated on any developments."

Julian arose and left the room. Jay and George, in turn, stood and accepted Hood's handshake, but in a manner the sheriff deemed perfunctory.

"I'll see you out," Anne said, as she fell into step beside him.

As they walked to the door, Hood heard the sound of a motor starting, followed by a screeching of tires. Outdoors, they stopped at the top of the stone steps and watched Julian's truck disappear from sight.

"Sorry about my brother," Anne said.

Hood wasn't sure which one she meant. "Don't be," he said. "This is a difficult time for your family."

"Still."

Hood was unable to read her expression. To pre-empt a repeat of the unanticipated greeting, he swiveled his head to look at the vehicles in the circular drive. "That's a nice 'Vette," he said. "Is it Jay's?"

"No. It's George's, but be careful if you bring it up. It's

become a sore point between George and Jay."

"How so?"

"Jay's always needling George about buying the 'Vette to compensate for his insecurities, and George doesn't take it well. My younger brother is very sensitive to criticism and he takes the bait every time, which only encourages Jay. Growing up, Henry and I learned not to tease George because he has such a thin skin, but Jay persists. It's funny, because those two are alike in so many ways."

Hood was intrigued by her insights and was framing a question to learn more about the family dynamic when Anne said, "Well, I'd better get back inside."

CHAPTER 8

"I've got to be honest with you, Francis," Otto Kampeter said, "as your campaign manager, I'm worried."

"Don't be," Hood said, hoping he sounded reassuring. He sat across from his brother-in-law in a booth at Millie's Diner, where a waitress had positioned a cup of coffee in front of each man. "The primary is still a month away."

"Less than a month—twenty-nine days, to be exact," Otto said. "And we have a lot to do."

Hood knew Otto was being kind with his use of the word "we." Otto had done most of the work. He had rounded up homeowners who agreed to display yard signs. He had assembled volunteers to put up the signs, hang placards on front doors, and distribute flyers at parish picnics and other community events. He also had courted financial donors and amassed a substantial campaign fund to purchase promotional items and advertising.

"I'm going to pick up the pace," Hood said, largely to ease his own guilt about his indolent role in their partnership. He recalled the words of his sponsor, Matthew, who had said, "I can only share my experience in sobriety. You have to do the work." Hood was realistic about his aversion to campaigning, but he also realized doing more work would ease his conscience, as well as help him keep his job.

"Good to hear," Otto said. He blew across his cup and sipped coffee. "On another matter, Grindell's ad claims violent crime in the county has—what was the word he used?—surged. That doesn't sound right to me."

"I've thought about that, too. All I can figure is the numbers have been pretty low, but we had that triple-homicide a few years back and maybe that skewed the figures."

"I'll check it out," Otto said. "Those reports are public records, right?"

"Yes. Ask Maggie."

Otto nodded as he swirled the remainder of the coffee in his cup. "I'm sure Linda mentioned Sarah and I are hosting our annual barbecue Saturday."

"Looking forward to it." Hood was sincere. The family gathering at Otto and Sarah's extensive property featured sumptuous barbeque, good company, outdoor games, and fishing and pony rides for the kids.

"I've invited a friend, a wealthy potential donor, but he wants to meet you and have a conversation before he commits."

Hood trusted Otto, but didn't trust potential donors who wanted a *conversation*—which Hood translated as quid pro quo—before contributing money.

Otto apparently interpreted Hood's silent misgivings because he added, "He's a straight-shooter, Francis. He's not going to ask for anything—certainly nothing, you know, shady. I wouldn't do that."

"I know," Hood said. He experienced newfound guilt

about his failure to trust Otto's judgment.

"He's a law-and-order guy, and we both know that's the base Grindell is targeting, but I sense my friend is not on the same page with your opponent. He just wants to know where you stand on some things." Otto sipped coffee. "I'm just asking you to meet him and hear him out."

"Of course," Hood said, hoping his assurance included a tacit apology. "I'll be there."

"Good."

Hood rotated his ceramic cup on the table top. "Anything else?"

"I know how you feel about politics, Francis. I knew that before I agreed to manage your campaign. I want you to know I'm not complaining. I just want to remind you what's at stake and ask you to step up."

Hood nodded.

"Okay," Otto said. "Pep talk's over."

Hood felt uneasy. Unable to pinpoint the source, he considered it must be his upcoming meeting—in less than an hour—with Anne.

He had wanted to interview Anne first and she had agreed, so why, he asked himself, was he apprehensive? Although Anne had implied she and her mother agreed to disavow the shared family alibi, it was Anne who delivered the message during their conversation at the Trestle.

And, as Jay had pointed out, Anne's unique memory

could provide details that might be useful in subsequent interviews with other family members.

He contemplated a timeline for the remaining interviews. He decided Marjorie, the matriarch, or Anne's younger brother, Henry, would be next. Jay and George would come later. Last would be Jay's wife Diane, who might be the most tangential to the case, and Julian, who might be the most hostile.

He glanced at his wall clock and realized it was time to leave.

Hood arrived at Anne's house five minutes before the appointed time. Punctuality was among his virtues; he considered it rude to keep others waiting.

Anne had designed and supervised construction of her home—more modest than ostentatious—in a newer subdivision a real estate professional might characterize as upper middle-class. Hood managed only a cursory glance at the tidy, functional rooms as she led him to the kitchen.

"Coffee?" she asked.

"Please," Hood said. He sat at a rectangular, glass-topped table centered in the kitchen. "Did you get to write down what we talked about?"

"Yes," she said. She pressed a button on the coffee maker, starting the brewing process.

"I heard you're working for a non-profit agency." Hood said, as the gurgling, percolating sounds began.

"Yes, the Mid-Missouri Adoption and Foster Care Program.

The name pretty much says it. We work to place children with adoptive or foster families." Anne remained standing at the counter as the coffee brewed. "When they age out of the system, we try to link them to employment opportunities, housing, social services, and so on. As you can imagine, a lot of what we do is communication and promotion."

"Sounds like quite a change from being an accountant."

"It is," Anne said. "Father wanted me to become a CPA, so I could be the newspaper's bookkeeper. That was one of his peculiarities—keeping the family business within the family. As you know, all of us children worked there." She removed two cups from a cabinet. "At least, we all did before Henry left, then me."

"After your father disappeared," Hood said.

"Ah," Anne said, "I can almost hear the gears turning in your head—a son and stepdaughter resign positions at family business after Father disappears. How suspicious is that? Did they feel pressured to join the newspaper?" she asked, making teasing air quotes with her fingers. "Are they resentful?"

"Are you?" Hood asked.

"I can't speak for my brother, but no, I'm not. I'm a realist. I enjoyed my time at college—all expenses paid, thanks to my parents—and I was grateful to have a job without having to subject myself to the whole arbitrary, anxiety-inducing interview process. We had a good team at the newspaper and my work was challenging. I certainly don't look back on those years as wasted time. I see them as the foundation for the life I enjoy today—this house, a healthy savings account, my BMW."

"So why'd you leave?"

"New opportunities." The coffee maker quieted. Anne filled the cups and set one before Hood, then sat perpendicular to him at the table. "While I was in college, I volunteered to work with underprivileged children and I realized that was my passion. And then, of course, there was Julian. Father and Mother took him in as a foster child, and he and I developed, I don't know, a bond."

Hood sipped coffee. "How so?"

"It's hard to describe," she said, "but I knew he was troubled."

Hood watched Anne's expression change as she transitioned to another time and place.

"There was this one time," she continued. "It was in 1996, Oct. 19, a Saturday. I was at the house that afternoon when Julian came home from school as angry as I'd ever seen him. Apparently, someone had punctured a tire on this junker car father had given him. Julian had never had much as a kid and this beater was his first car. He put every cent he earned into fixing it up.

"A few days later, a couple, along with their teenage son, knocked on the door and asked to speak with my parents. They said their kid's dog was hurt and their vet said someone severed a tendon on the dog's hind leg. The vet said the cut was intentional, not an accident. Anyway, things got very accusatory, and heated, and the couple left with threats of legal action that never happened."

"Did Julian ever say he did it?"

"He denied it, vehemently, but I never believed him." She lifted her cup slightly, then returned it to the tabletop. "And you know what scared me the most?"

Hood remained silent, aware the question was rhetorical.

"Julian didn't retaliate against the kid, he went after the dog. It was so cruel, like some mobster vendetta you read about."

"Kids can be cruel," Hood said, immediately regretting how trite his words sounded.

"I think I've always felt I could have done more for Julian," Anne said. "I tried to talk to him, be the big sister, but there was the age gap—I was five years older. Plus, I was working full time, so we didn't get to spend much time together. The next thing I knew—he was gone."

"Do you keep in touch?"

"I try but I don't seem to do a very good job of it. We don't have much in common as adults and we've drifted apart, but it's sad. I guess you could say that Julian—and the foster kids I worked with during college—changed my heart."

Hood waited silently as Anne sipped coffee, then Anne reached for a yellow legal pad on a corner of the table and handed it to him. "Here's the timeline you requested," she said.

"Thanks," Hood tilted the pad at an upward angle and read:

"On August 11, I arrived at my parents' home at 9:28 a.m. to begin preparing our family dinner. I recall the time because I looked at the digital clock on the kitchen wall. The dinner is routinely held at 1 p.m. on Sundays and attended by all immediate family members who are available.

I used my key to let myself in because Mother and Henry, who was living at home at the time, usually sleep late on Sunday and mother had texted me Saturday evening and informed me Father planned to leave the house early in the morning.

On that day, I was making vegetarian lasagna, partially because it's one of Mother's and Henry's favorites, but also because I knew Jay—who had been an ass lately—hated meatless meals.

I knew I had plenty of time to prepare, but also knew I had a lot to do. I like to make my lasagna noodles from scratch and there're a lot of vegetables to chop, plus I planned to serve a salad with olives, cucumbers, and garbanzo beans.

Mother keeps a well-stocked kitchen as far as staples and spices go, but I had stopped at the Shop' N' Save on the way over to buy fresh vegetables. I unpacked and washed the green pepper, tomatoes, and celery, and peeled and washed the carrots and zucchini.

I noticed Mother's kitchen towels had cherries, which I found ironic because I wasn't preparing a fruit salad, which I often do.

As I write this, my memory is pulling me into some stream-of-consciousness mode, so I'll try to stick to what matters.

Mother, trailed by her puppy, Danielle, came into the kitchen about a half-hour after I arrived. I didn't look at the clock, but it was while I was kneading the pasta dough, which I decided to do before chopping the veggies. She poured herself a cup of coffee, fed Danielle, and went to the sunroom, which is separated from the kitchen by the dining room.

THE FORGET-ME-KNOT

I had finished rolling and cutting the noodles and was chopping celery when Henry came into the kitchen. I did glance up at the clock, which read 10:05. I presumed Henry had just gotten out of bed, because he wore a robe, looked groggy, and immediately poured himself coffee. We shared a hug and brief conversation before he excused himself and left. Shortly after, I heard an upstairs shower running.

George arrived sometime after noon. I didn't check the clock, but I knew it was after noon, because I had already popped the lasagna in the oven. He didn't come in the kitchen or greet me, but I knew he was in the house because I overheard him talking with mother in the sunroom.

About 12:30 p.m., during a lull in the action while the lasagna was cooking, I went into the dining room to set the table and fill water glasses. Mother, George, and Henry—who had joined them—were talking in the sunroom, and I overheard Mother fretting about how long Father had been gone, while the boys reassured her he would be home on time because he was never late.

The timer buzzed and I returned to the kitchen for the final preparations. At 12:55 p.m., just as the lasagna had finished cooling and was ready to be served, I heard Jay come in. He routinely arrived at events or appointments with little time to spare. His reasoning was that his time was valuable, and waiting was a waste of time.

Just as I was about to carry the main course to the dining room, Mother entered the kitchen and told me Father hadn't returned yet. She said she had called his cell twice but received no answer.

We decided to put dinner on hold. I returned the lasagna to the oven at a warming temperature. After repeated phone calls and texts to father, Jay and George drove to the development site. They reported father's car was there, but there was no sign of him. They said they were going to look around and call back.

Mother, Henry, and I discussed possible reasons for his absence, but the conversation seemed to make her more distraught. Jay called Mother's cell, said they had found nothing more, and were heading back.

Before they returned, Henry and I talked Mother into lying down. When my two brothers arrived home, we continued calling Father's cell while discussing what to do next. Mother awakened at some point and rejoined the conversation, and we finally decided to call you."

The written narrative ended.

Hood took a notebook and pen from his pocket. "When we talked at the Trestle, you said it was your mother who had suggested the family alibi that you were all together at the house before your father left that morning."

"It was her idea, but it doesn't matter. We all agreed to it." Anne looked into her coffee cup, which was nearly empty. "I think her motives were pure. She wanted to protect us. She couldn't believe any of her children were involved and, quite frankly, neither could I."

Hood frowned. He resisted the urge to scold her for participating in the lie. He knew she was feeling remorse, and nothing would be gained by pointing out the family members' self-interest had all but scuttled a timely investigation of the disappearance.

"Was building a new printing plant your father's idea?"

Anne hesitated, and Hood watched her close her eyes and concentrate, almost as if replaying a tape in her mind.

"Now that you mention it," Anne said, "I don't actually know whose idea it was. I remember the first time I heard about it was when Jay introduced it as new business during a monthly board meeting. That was the morning of June 10, more than a year ago. But I don't know if he discussed it with Father or anyone else before that."

"What was the reaction from the other board members?"

"I was lukewarm. I think Henry was, too. It just seemed like a lot of money to spend. Father, and I think George, weren't exactly gung ho, but they seemed willing to explore the long-term viability."

"Has anyone brought up the idea of selling the newspaper?"

Anne chuffed a brief laugh. "When I was a kid, Sheriff, I thought my parents' house was a castle and I was a princess. But growing up amid wealth and power isn't all it's cracked up to be. Don't get me wrong, I'm grateful my family owns a multi-million dollar asset, but it's also a huge responsibility. The industry has transformed during my lifetime. Competition is fierce and it's not going away. Has the thought of selling the paper crossed my mind? Of course. I'm sure it's crossed everyone's mind at one time or other, but there are other considerations."

"Such as?"

"I can't speak for the others, and I've probably said too much already."

"Fair enough," Hood said. "Going back to before your father's disappearance, did you notice any changes in his behavior?"

"Not particularly."

"What about your Mother and siblings? Any noticeable changes in behavior leading up to or on the morning of the disappearance?"

"Nothing out of the ordinary. Jay and George were their usual self-absorbed selves. Henry seemed preoccupied with an offer to work with a theater group in Florida. Mother was flustered, but no more than usual."

"Based on what I saw the other day, you and your mom seem pretty close."

"We always have been. Growing up, Mother was very nurturing. As I'm sure you know, James is not my natural father, but he's been my stepfather for as long as I can remember. He tries, but he can be very demanding. I spent much of my youth trying to please him and I'm sure it was a factor in my decision to join the family business. Being a Bishop can be grueling."

"What about your brothers? Do you think they joined the business—at least, in part—to please your father?"

"I think they felt even more pressure than I did. Because of my hyperthymesia, I think my father saw me as some blend of freak and genius. I don't mean this to be unkind, but Father was kind of sexist when it came to the business. I think he saw me as a useful addition, but it was the boys, *his* children, he was grooming for *leadership*."

"The role Jay has stepped into."

"Jay is actually short for James Jr., which is exactly what he is—a younger version of Father. I appreciate material things, but James is absolutely driven by them—money, status, power." She sipped the last of her coffee. "You met his wife, Diane, the other day?"

Hood nodded.

"I don't mean this as criticism, but she checks all the boxes for a trophy wife. She's smart, fashion-conscious, and sophisticated, but none of that stops Jay from flirting with Veronica, his secretary—or, as he insists on calling her, his administrative assistant. It's shameful, really."

Hood wrote in his notebook.

"Look, I'm not saying there's anything going on," Anne said. "It may just be Jay's way of keeping his ego inflated."

"I understand Henry's in Florida," Hood said, "but he lived at home and worked in the family business until after your father disappeared, right?"

"I'd rather you talk to Henry about that."

Hood made a mental note of Anne's willingness to talk about Jay, but her reluctance to discuss Henry. "What about George?"

"What about him?"

"I understand he's held various positions at the newspaper."

"Father said the reassignments were about trying to find the right fit for George, to help him achieve his maximum potential with the company."

"What do you say?"

"I really shouldn't be talking about my family."

"I understand. I don't mean to make you uncomfortable, but things have changed. This is now a homicide investigation. I'm not asking you to betray a confidence. It's just that I've heard George can be difficult."

"That's a kind way to put it."

"How would you put it?"

"He's defensive, abrasive, and has a hair-trigger temper. If a customer has a complaint about anything, George takes it as a personal criticism and fires back. Father kept trying to find a place where George could contribute without creating conflict."

"Did he?"

"Before he disappeared, Father moved him to production manager, where he deals primarily with the press crew and newspaper distribution. I'm told the morale is low, but Jay puts up with it."

"Is Jay George's boss?"

"He is now—on paper, at least—although George will deny it. Jay knows how to schmooze George and get what he wants, so he doesn't make it a thing."

"How do you and George get along?"

"Better, now that we're not co-workers. He's my brother and I love him, but—" she finished her coffee, stood, and rinsed her cup in the sink. Without turning to face Hood, she said, "I really feel like I'm talking too much."

Hood sensed it was time to stop. "Thanks. You've been very helpful."

Anne turned and focused on his cup. "Are you finished?"

"I guess I am."

CHAPTER 9

Hood stopped at the gate to the Bishop estate. He leaned toward the intercom to announce his arrival and was surprised when Anne's voice greeted him.

He had arranged to interview Marjorie and expected their conversation to be private.

Anne seemed to sense his confusion because, when she met him at the top of the stone steps, she explained, almost apologetically, that her mother had asked her to "sit in."

Hood followed Anne to the family room, where Marjorie was seated with her puppy curled beside her on the sofa. After exchanging greetings, Hood and Anne sat in matching chairs facing Marjorie.

"Did you get a chance to write what you remember about the morning your husband disappeared?" Hood asked.

"I tried." Marjorie handed the sheriff a single sheet of paper. "It's not much. I'm not sure I'll be much help."

Hood read what she had written. Her notes contained no new information and nothing that was inconsistent with Anne's account.

"I understand the shared alibi was your idea."

Marjorie nodded.

"Why did you propose it?"

"It seemed like a good idea at that time—for everybody. I knew my children weren't involved, so the alibi would spare them from being suspected or questioned in their own father's disappearance. But, beyond that, I thought it would keep the investigation on track. I mean, if the family members were eliminated as suspects, the case would stay focused on what really happened."

"But you recently recanted the alibi?" Hood framed the remark as a question instead of a statement.

"Yes."

"Why?"

"I don't know. Maybe I'm tired of not knowing." She looked through an oversized window, its glass filmy. "Maybe I wanted you to reopen the investigation."

"You know I'll be investigating everything—every possibility and every person. Do you still believe none of the children was involved?"

"I want to."

Hood leaned forward. "I'm sensing doubt."

"Every family has problems. You might think that since we want for nothing, everyone would be satisfied, but sometimes it seems just the opposite."

Hood nodded, encouraging her to continue.

"My husband wanted the children to join the business," Marjorie continued. "I think he considered it his legacy, his gift to them."

"But," Hood prompted.

"Some wanted it, some didn't."

Hood considered what Anne had said about being born into wealth. "Did your husband discuss the future of the business with you?"

"Oh, yes. I think he used me as a sounding board because I could offer a balanced perspective. These are troubling times in the newspaper industry and they were troubling times for James. From a business standpoint, he saw an industry being eaten alive. He worried about hanging on until only a carcass remained for his children. But from an emotional perspective, he couldn't let go. He didn't want to be the one who abandoned the Bishop family's legacy of documenting local history."

"Is that why he was planning to build a new printing plant and scouting potential sites?"

"I wouldn't exactly say he was planning it. He was considering it, but hadn't decided whether to move forward."

"Whose idea was it to build the new plant?"

"I don't know if it was Jay's idea, but he was the main proponent. Wouldn't you agree, dear?" Marjorie asked Anne, who nodded.

"Would it be fair to say Jay was next in line to—how do I put it—oversee operations at the newspaper?"

"Was he the heir apparent, you mean?" Marjorie asked.

"Was he?"

"Now we're getting into family matters," Marjorie said. "Right now, Jay and I share management responsibilities as determined by our board of directors."

"The board is you and your four children, correct?" Hood asked.

"Yes."

"And two of them—Anne and Henry—no longer work at the newspaper but remain on the board."

"Is that a question?" Marjorie asked.

Hood heard a bristle in her tone. Not wanting their exchange to become confrontational, he adopted a more conversational approach. "Anne and I have discussed her career change, but what can you tell me about Henry's decision?"

"He was never interested in any of his parents' pursuits," she said. "As you may recall, Sheriff, I once was a champion marksman—competed throughout the Midwest. After I became a mother, I tried to interest each of my children in the sport, but Henry wanted no part of it. He also wanted no part in my husband's pursuits, including the business. He'd rather sit in his room all day writing song lyrics and playing our piano or instruments he borrowed from the school's music program."

"But wasn't he the ad manager before he moved away?" Hood asked.

"In body, but not in spirit. James tailored the position for Henry, hoping his son would be attracted to the challenge, or the money, or the power, but it never happened. Henry actually was quite good at his job. He's intelligent and personable, but I knew he hated every minute of managing the sales reps and wooing advertisers. He preferred writing songs or working on a musical."

"I thought he majored in business," Hood said.

"He did," Anne answered, "but only to please Father.

After he received his degree from Cornell—that's in Ithaca, New York—he told Father he wanted to stay on the East Coast. He said he'd met a girl and he wanted to chill for a while. What he didn't tell Father was that he got accepted to a pretty prestigious music school."

Hood recalled Henry had left the family business and relocated to Florida. "I understand Henry moved away. When exactly was that?"

"It wasn't long after—" Marjorie began.

"He told us on August 26," Anne said. "It was the Monday, two weeks after Father's August 11 disappearance. Henry left here September 9, also a Monday, two weeks after he gave notice."

"I was surprised he stayed as long as he did," Marjorie said. "After he told us he'd accepted the job offer in Florida, he was like a racehorse in the starting gate, waiting for it to open so he could bolt." She looked to her daughter. "It was hard on you, wasn't it dear? You and Henry were always close."

"Henry and I both appreciated the opportunities you and Father made available to us, but we each had a passion to pursue other things." Anne turned to Hood. "The sheriff and I already have gone over my career change," she said.

Hood sensed a finality in her tone. He refocused on Marjorie. "How did your husband and Jay get along?"

"Fine," Marjorie answered, as if the monosyllable said it all.

"No differences over business matters, no quarrels, no—"

"I can see why you might think that, but Jay was very respectful. He knew he was being groomed. He didn't need to compete."

"And what about George?"

"Oh, Georgie," Marjorie said, plaintively. "Some young people have difficulty finding themselves. Things just haven't worked out for him, yet. I think he just gets frustrated sometimes."

"As I understand it, he's been reassigned to various—"

"I know what you're getting at, Sheriff." Marjorie scooted forward, momentarily disturbing the puppy's nap. "Do you have children, Sheriff?"

"Just one. A daughter."

"I wouldn't know about an only child, but based on my experience, the oldest and youngest face unique challenges. Georgie's the youngest, you know. I think he's always felt overshadowed by his siblings."

Hood glanced at Anne, then refocused on Marjorie. "Can you describe Anne's challenges as the oldest?"

"Oh, heavens," she said. "Anne's biggest challenge was not being the oldest, it was being the only daughter, as well as my husband's only stepchild. James was old school, Sheriff. He never envisioned her running the newspaper."

Marjorie turned to her daughter, as did Hood, who noticed Anne seemed absorbed in her own musings.

"Anne knows this," Marjorie continued." We talked about it when she was growing up. She was groomed to play a role, but not the leadership role. That was always reserved for Jay."

"The sheriff and I have already discussed this," Anne said, her attention abruptly returning to the conversation.

"Okay," Hood said, sensing Anne's desire to change the

topic. "What can you tell me about Julian?"

"I'd rather not talk about Julian. He was only with us for a short time, and that was years ago. Besides, you investigated him the first time around."

Hood turned to Anne, hoping for her assistance, but her expression suggested he drop the topic.

The sheriff looked at his notebook, then asked, "Did you notice any changes in your husband's attitude or behavior in the days prior to his disappearance?"

"No. Nothing noticeable."

"What about the children—anything unusual about them leading up to or on the morning of the disappearance?"

Marjorie shook her head. "No. It was just a typical week with a typical Sunday morning. I was a little puzzled by Henry's walk that morning, but after he explained it—"

"Was he limping or something?"

"Oh, no Sheriff. Not the way he walked. He took a walk. Early that morning."

A pulse of adrenalin heightened Hood's attentiveness. "The morning your husband disappeared?" he asked, seeking clarification.

"Yes, I was upstairs. I was getting dressed to come downstairs and I looked out the window and saw him on the walkway to the back door."

"Did either of you see him when he came in?"

"No," Marjorie answered. "He must have gone directly to his room."

"I was in the kitchen," Anne said. "I never heard the back door open."

"I asked him about it later that morning," Marjorie added. "He said he woke up early and decided to go for a walk."

"Did he routinely take walks in the morning?"

"No," Marjorie said. "He said he was having trouble sleeping lately."

Hood looked to Anne, whose expression revealed confusion and concern. She shook her head.

"I'm sure it was just a walk," Marjorie said. "I believe him. He couldn't have had anything to do with the disappearance. He wouldn't. I'm his mother. I would know." She stood. "I'm going to lie down."

Defensiveness, now denial, Hood thought, remembering how he had sought refuge in denial when he was an active alcoholic. He stood as well. "I'll be in touch."

Anne escorted him outside. "Thanks for not making a thing about me being here today," she said. "It was Mother's wish."

Hood wasn't sure her presence had made any difference. He also saw no gain in objecting now. "It's fine," he said.

"It was good to see you again," she said.

Hood intentionally stepped back to avoid a repeat of the brief kiss she had greeted him with during their previous encounter. Instead, he extended his hand and Anne shook it.

As he drove away, he wondered whether the moment was awkward.

THE FORGET-ME-KNOT

* * * * *

Julian set the oversized, right rear tire against the racetrack's dirt "cushion" and turned the sprint car into a power slide.

Car owner Ed McCullough and mechanic Rusty Koenigsfeld watched from the infield as the No. 11 sprayed a plume of dark soil against the white retaining wall in the first turn.

Julian steered onto the back straightaway and, again, fell in just behind race leader Stevie Steedman's No. 3.

"Damn," Ed said. "If Julian keeps runnin' that high groove, he'll never catch Stevie."

"It's a two-groove track," Rusty said. "That upper cushion is fast, but it's the long way around. If Stevie stays low, he'll be hard to pass."

"Passin' low is risky as hell," Ed said, referring to the perils of contact for the open-wheeled, high-horsepower race cars. "I'd like the trophy, but not if means tearin' up the car."

Ed was aware "tearin' up the car" was a distinct possibility. He knew Julian could be reckless, particularly when he was losing to one of the so-called kids. Among those kids was Stevie, 16-year-old son of former national champion Butch Steedman. During the long drives from one track to another, Ed had endured Julian's rants about second-generation adolescents who were dominating the sport, at the expense—literally—of the more veteran campaigners. "It pisses me off," Julian had complained. "We paid our dues, worked our way up, while these snot-nosed kids are being handed the best cars and most powerful motors daddy's money can buy."

Ed and Rusty lost sight of the leaders until they exited turn four, with Stevie still leading but Julian seemingly attached to his rear nerf bar. The grandstand and white flag, signaling the final lap, passed in a blur as Julian carved into the lowest possible groove of the first turn.

For a moment, the two cars appeared as one until Julian's car fishtailed slightly, tapped Stevie's tire and sent the No. 3 into a cartwheel. The youngster's racer somersaulted twice, careened into the guardrail and retaining wall, then bounded onto its wheels and settled.

Ed and Rusty watched their driver take the checkered flag, followed by his victory lap, which included a gloved, single-finger salute from Stevie, who remained in the first turn awaiting assistance for his damaged car.

After the trophy presentation, the three men stood in the pit near the enclosed trailer where Julian had parked the car for transport. The men were drinking celebratory beers when Butch Steedman crashed their party, backing Julian into the trailer.

"You're a fucking asshole." Butch shouted, his face only inches from Julian's.

Ed intervened immediately, inserting himself in the narrow space between the two men. "Whoa, whoa," Ed said. "We were just racin', man."

"He put my kid in the wall," Butch spat.

Ed knew Butch was enraged, but he was encouraged that no punches had been thrown, yet. The two men had competed on the sprint car circuit for nearly two decades and, although they were rivals, they were not enemies.

"The high groove wasn't working. We had to go low. The contact wasn't intentional. Julian could just as easily have spun himself."

"Bullshit," Butch said.

Ed put up his hands in a defensive gesture. "Julian, tell him it was just a bobble, accidental contact."

"If your kid can't take a love tap," Julian said. "He oughta go back to go-karts."

Chaos erupted. Legs kicked. Arms flailed. All three men tumbled to the ground in a tangle of punches, grunts, and screeches reminiscent of a fight among feral cats.

CHAPTER 10

"What should I wear?" Hood asked his wife as he stood in his underwear and peered into the open closet.

"Why don't you wear your uniform," Linda said, more a suggestion than a question.

"I don't know. It seems a little—" he hesitated, then added, "unfair, I guess."

"You *are* the sheriff," Linda said. "Besides, you hate suits."

"What I hate is having to make a command performance before the Republican faithful and beg for their endorsement to keep my job."

Linda made no reply. She already had advised her husband that challenger Steve Grindell—and his handler, Chip Luther—had been courting the party leadership. Although attending the event might be unpleasant—perhaps, at times, confrontational—declining the invitation would be tantamount to political suicide.

"I think I'll go with the suit," Hood said. He kept his gaze fixed on the closet to avoid Linda's look of disapproval, then pulled the dark suit from its hanger.

While he dressed, Linda sat on the bed, focused on nothing in particular.

Hood's thoughts continued to center on the day's

frustrations, including his failure to reach Henry Bishop and his snit with his dispatcher, Maggie.

Despite his repeated reminders to avoid obsessive thinking, his mind refused to obey. Questions he would ask Henry began to form even before the conclusion of yesterday's interview with Marjorie. Sleep had eluded Hood the previous night as he contemplated how to get the most from a phone interview with Henry.

In the morning, mindful of the time change, Hood had called and left a message on Henry's answering machine. He had busied himself with paperwork as he stewed impatiently, awaiting a return call. When none came, he skulked to the dispatcher's station. He had asked Maggie to find out if the Bishops had owned their current vehicles at the time the patriarch vanished. He requested an update, the impatience in his tone apparent.

When Maggie said she hadn't received an answer yet, he scolded her. Although he apologized immediately for his display of frustration, his mood continued to worsen throughout the afternoon.

He brightened somewhat when Maggie later called and—in a more cordial conversation showing she harbored no ill will—informed her boss that the Bishop children's ownership of their vehicles predated the disappearance, making them available to be searched if necessary. Nevertheless, the workday had ended with the annoyance of failing to reach Henry coupled with the anxiety of an evening facing county Republicans.

Hood forced a smile, faced himself in the full-length mirror and straightened his suit coat. "How do I look?" he asked Linda.

"Very handsome."

"I was going for authoritative."

"That, too."

In the moment he turned to look at her, he realized he had been focusing entirely on himself—his concerns, his frustrations, his appearance. His recovery program emphasized humility, and although he embraced the theory, he hadn't modeled the behavior. He tried to recall the last time he had done something, or even said something, to show his affection.

He repeatedly had told his recovery sponsor he was grateful his family had reunited, but he hadn't demonstrated his gratitude to his wife or, for that matter, his daughter.

He glanced at his watch and noted it was time to go. As he walked down the stair, he resolved to do better.

Hood sat in a metal folding chair in a hallway at the Huhman County Republican Committee headquarters.

As usual, he had arrived early and had shared a greeting or brief conversation with committee members as they arrived and entered the designated meeting room.

Hood noticed his primary challenger, Steve Grindell, pacing in the foyer, apparently biding his time before the interview.

Hood waited impatiently until the door to the meeting room was opened from within and Grindell's name was called.

Grindell avoided eye contact with Hood as he approached and disappeared into the room. The door closed, leaving the sheriff alone in the corridor.

He sat silently for a while, tapped his foot, stood, and paced the length of the hallway. He repeated his routine—sit, tap, pace—innumerable times before the door reopened.

Grindell emerged, mumbled "Good luck" to Hood, and exited hurriedly.

Hood entered the room and sat in the lone, unoccupied, uncomfortable folding chair facing eleven of the committee's twelve delegates who had gathered to consider the party's endorsement.

He massaged his scalp and the back of his neck. The room was a little too claustrophobic for his liking, the temperature a touch too warm, and the frowning expression of Mrs. Maupin a tad too austere. He recalled that his wife had identified Mrs. Maupin as one of the dissenters, and although the GOP stalwart no longer served as committee chairwoman, she remained revered as the party's matriarch.

Hood tugged at the knot in his tie and scanned the faces of the other committee members. He had received pledges of support from four, he counted three as Grindell supporters, and the other four he suspected were undecided. The absent delegate seemed to favor Hood but had made no commitment to the sheriff.

The evening began with the chairman's welcome and introduction, followed by benign questions about campaign progress and Hood's priorities, if elected.

The delegates took turns posing questions, all of which Hood had anticipated and considered. He became increasingly confident that his familiarity with the workings of the agency provided him an advantage over his challenger.

When the questioning eventually turned to Mrs. Maupin, she focused on the sheriff and said, "Mr. Hood, tell us how you think your tenure as sheriff has helped further the interests of the Republican Party."

He hesitated. "I'm not sure what you mean, exactly."

"I mean what I said. You've been sheriff now for what—nine years? How have you furthered the interests of the Republican Party?"

Hood detected a trace of self-satisfied curtness in her tone. He straightened in his chair. He sensed he was being set up but couldn't foresee the direction of the attack. He reached again to tug at the knot in his tie, then decided against displaying his increasing discomfort.

"I would say," he began, choosing his words carefully, "that I've always tried to be a good sheriff. I've tried to be conscientious and fair. And to the extent that I'm a Republican, I would hope that perception among voters also helps other Republican office-holders and candidates."

"Your opponent," Mrs. Maupin said, "pointed out that the sheriff's department, at this time, employs forty-two people, including deputies, jailers, dispatchers, process servers, and clerical staff. He also said he was certain there are people affiliated with the Republican Party who are well-qualified to be recommended for those positions—and to fill them—as vacancies become available."

Hood closed his eyes momentarily and focused on the innuendo. Although he wasn't sure how or when, he sensed one of his hirings or promotions had displeased Mrs. Maupin. "May I respond?" he asked, his indignation apparent.

"Please do," Mrs. Maupin said.

"The first priority of the sheriff's department is the safety and welfare of the residents of this county," Hood said. "My first priority is to ensure the people who work for this department are the most professional, most dedicated, and most qualified." He paused and took a long breath to compose himself. "All other things being equal, I don't disagree with what Mr. Grindell told you. But if the choice is between a good deputy and a good Republican, I'm here to tell you this county will have a good deputy."

"Well said," Mrs. Maupin replied. "Then I take it you feel you have a corps of good deputies."

"Yes, I do."

"Given that you have so many well-qualified deputies, Mr. Hood, would you explain to this committee why you selected Gus Wallendorf to serve as your chief deputy, in view of his affiliation with the Democratic party?"

The question staggered Hood. Although he had anticipated some type of ambush, he was caught entirely off guard. His thoughts whirled and collided as he struggled for some type of explanation.

"We're waiting, Mr. Hood."

"I'm not sure I know exactly what—"

"Mr. Wallendorf serves as a Democratic representative on a city committee," Mrs. Maupin said. "I'm sure you're aware—"

"Oh, that," Hood said.

"Yes, that," Mrs. Maupin repeated, with emphasis.

"That's just—he's just—the city had a vacancy on its Police Personnel Board, and they asked Wally to serve. The board's pretty nonpartisan, but the rules require an even split between Republicans and Democrats. The vacancy was for a Democrat. Wally's mostly independent as far as politics go, but the city said it wouldn't be a problem, so he joined."

"As a Democrat," Mrs. Maupin added.

"Yes, but—"

"I don't see any buts about it," Mrs. Maupin interrupted. "The man you elevated to be your chief deputy is on the public record as a Democrat, and here you are asking this committee for its endorsement."

Hood exhaled a long breath, recalling his campaign manager's words: "When you're explaining or defending, you're losing." He surveyed the faces of the committee members, focusing on Mrs. Maupin's smug expression. Otto, he realized, was right. He was defending, and he definitely was losing.

Think through the drink.

The slogan, popular in Hood's recovery program, echoed in the sheriff's mind.

He sat behind the wheel of his vehicle, parked in the

convenience store lot, and stared through the window at the shelves of liquor bottles and glass-doored coolers of cold beer.

When he left the meeting with the Republican committee, he knew he wanted a drink. He told himself he didn't *need* a drink, he just wanted one.

One drink. Just one to calm his edginess.

What he did need was to fill his gas tank, so he drove to At Your Convenience. After the nozzle had clicked and he pocketed his receipt, however, he had parked at the storefront rather than driving home.

But he hadn't gone inside.

Yet.

He recalled a similar scenario when he was about two months sober. He had developed a resentment to comments from his sister-in-law, Sarah, and had found himself in the parking lot of Good Times Liquor Store. He had paced around the lot until he finally called Matthew, his sponsor in recovery. On that occasion, Matthew had urged him to meet for coffee and he agreed.

Hood removed his cell phone and scrolled through his contact list until Matthew's number appeared. He stared at it but didn't press call. Did he really need to call? Back then, he rationalized, he was relatively new to recovery; now, he was approaching a year of sobriety. He didn't want to be a pest. Besides, he told himself, Matthew would probably just trot out another shopworn slogan, like *One drink is too many and a hundred is not enough.*

Hood already knew that. He knew one drink not only

would torpedo his months of continuous sobriety, it would also destroy any trust he had been rebuilding with his family and friends. He also knew he would regret his relapse and would feel compelled to admit it to his recovery group.

He started the ignition, backed out, and headed home.

Think through the drink.

The slogan worked.

CHAPTER 11

"This is Huhman County Sheriff Francis Hood calling from Missouri. Is Henry Bishop available?"

"Speaking."

"Henry," the sheriff said. "I know you were on speaker phone the other day when I talked with your family about your father's disappearance. I wanted to see if you'd had an opportunity to write what you remember about that time."

"It's almost finished. I was going to look it over and send it to you later today."

"Could you email it now?"

"I suppose."

"Do you have my email address?"

"Anne gave it to me."

"Good. Can I call you back after I've read it?"

"I've got rehearsal this afternoon."

"I'll make it a priority. If you send it right away, I'll get back to you within the hour."

"Okay."

"Thanks." Hood disconnected, walked to the coffee maker, and refilled his cup. When he returned and opened his email, Henry's message had arrived. He perused it carefully, focusing on a passage that read:

I was up early on the morning my father disappeared. I was still living at my family's home at the time and working at the newspaper. An opportunity arose to pursue my dream of scoring musical theater productions, but it would mean leaving my job and moving to Florida.

I won't bore you with the details, but I was torn about what to do, so much so that I was having trouble sleeping. I was awake before 5 a.m. and couldn't fall back asleep, so I decided to get up and take a walk.

I remember Dad had said he was planning to visit a possible site for a new printing plant. He even asked me the night before if I wanted to go with him, but I said no. I didn't hear anyone else up and around that early, but I wasn't in the house for long. I didn't shower or have breakfast or anything. I just put on clothes and went out through the garage. Dad's car was still there, so I knew he hadn't left yet. I was gone awhile, but when I got back, Anne's car was out front, Dad's car was gone, and I heard Mom upstairs in her room.

I climbed back in bed and, to my surprise, I was able to fall back to sleep. When I woke up the second time and went to get some coffee, Anne was in the kitchen cooking and Mom was in the sunroom. She was reading the Sunday paper and Danielle was in her lap. She said she saw me earlier and asked where I had been. All I said was I was having trouble sleeping and decided to go for a walk.

The inclusion of the early-morning walk in Henry's narrative surprised Hood. The walk was among the sheriff's few clues. It established opportunity for Henry to be involved in the disappearance and was, according to Marjorie, out of character. Nevertheless, Henry not only included it, he explained it. Perhaps, Hood considered, Henry did so because Marjorie or Anne had informed him the information already had been shared with the sheriff.

Hood returned Henry's call and said, "About this early morning walk, did you know I already had been made aware of that?"

"Yes," Henry replied. "Anne called yesterday and said my mom had mentioned it to you, so I put in the email. By the way, I meant to ask Anne if she told you about the stain in Jay's vehicle, but I forgot. Did she?"

"Stain?" Hood asked. "What kind of stain?

"I don't know if it was blood, but that's what it looked like. Anne and I were helping Jay load some boxes in the back of his Range Rover and we both saw it."

"This was after your father disappeared?"

"A couple weeks after," Henry said. "Anne will remember the date. At the time, I remember Anne and I looking at each other like we knew we shouldn't be thinking what we were thinking. It was unsettling, so I asked Jay about it, right then and there."

"And what did he say?"

"He said it was Dad's blood. Then he looked at our expressions and said something like, 'I can't believe you two.' He explained he and Dad were unloading a metal newspaper rack and Dad cut himself and started bleeding. Boy, did I feel like a jerk."

"So you believed him?"

"I did, and not just because of what he said, but how he said it. He answered right away. It wasn't like he needed time to make up some lie. Besides, the stain wasn't that big, it was more like a blot."

Or, Hood thought, Jay had formulated an answer in advance. "What about Anne? Did she believe the explanation?"

"You'll have to ask Anne about that."

Hood made a note. "Tell me more about this job offer that was weighing on you."

"I didn't know if the details were important," Henry said. "You asked us to write what we remembered about the morning Dad disappeared. What was on my mind back then was I had been offered an opportunity to help score the music for an original theater production."

Hood recalled Marjorie's description of her son's musical talents. "How did this opportunity come about?"

"Maybe I should start at the beginning. You probably know Dad wanted all us kids to join him in the business. My role was to manage the advertising department, so he arranged and paid for me to enroll in the business program at Cornell. That's in upstate New York."

"Yes, I know," Hood said.

"It's beautiful there, especially in the fall," Henry said. "Well, after I got my degree, I told my family I had met somebody. I said I wanted to stay in the area, see how the relationship developed, and just enjoy the scenery for a while. What I didn't tell them was I had been accepted into

Ithaca College's School of Music, which is pretty exclusive and prestigious.

"While I was there, a friend and I began writing songs together. We even collaborated on a one-act musical. We gained some notoriety in and around campus, but that was the extent of it. Eventually, I went home to Missouri and joined Dad's business and my friend took a job with a theater group in Florida.

"I didn't hear from him again until last summer when he called, said his company planned to start producing its own musicals, and asked me to collaborate with him. I was ecstatic. I wanted to do it—it's in my heart—but, at the same time, I didn't want to disappoint my dad."

"How did he react when you told him your decision?"

"I never did. He disappeared before I got the chance. I told my friend what had happened. He understood, but he also said he needed an answer by mid-September. I agonized over the decision, but in the end, I couldn't say no. I told the family and started making plans to leave."

"How did your mother react to your decision to relocate?"

"She seemed both happy and sad. I could tell she shared my joy, but I knew a part of her wanted me to stay."

"What about your brothers and stepsister?"

"Telling Anne was one of the hardest things about making the decision. I knew I was going to miss her. She was the one who always stood up for me."

"What about George?"

"I don't think he cared a bit. We were never that close."

"And Jay?"

"Jay knew I had made up my mind to leave, but he still acted all disappointed. He even tried to talk me out of it, but I could tell he was delighted to have one less Bishop to deal with in the company."

"Were you aware of any plans or discussion about building a new printing plant?"

"It was a topic at a board meeting."

"Whose idea was it?"

"I'm guessing it was Jay's. I know he supported it."

"Did you?"

"I was waiting to see cost estimates, site plans, that sort of thing before making a decision. But truth be told, I was thinking about Florida and hoping the project wouldn't come to a vote before I left."

"Why was that?"

"I thought it would create hard feelings with Jay if I opposed the project on my way out the door," Henry said. "Are we about done? I've got to get to rehearsal."

"Okay," Hood said. "But I may need to talk to you again."

"Sure."

After they disconnected, Hood looked at his notes. Below the words *blood stain,* he had written, *ask Jay* – and below that, *ask Anne.*

Hood was driving along the residential portion of St. Gotthard's West Main Street when he spotted Young John descending the porch steps of one of the stately two-story brick homes set well back from the street and shaded by two massive oak trees.

As the rookie deputy, who was not in uniform, turned onto the sidewalk, Hood noticed Young John was clutching a handful of pamphlets.

The sheriff pulled to the curb, got out, and approached. "Hey John," he greeted. "What's up?"

"Nothing," Young John said. He attempted to shield the leaflets behind his hip. "Just out walking."

"What've you got there?" Hood asked, gesturing toward the deputy's hidden hand.

"Just some handouts. Hey, while I've got you here, I wanted to—"

"C'mon John," Hood interrupted. He smiled. "You look like the kid who got caught with his hand in the cookie jar."

"Okay. You got me," Young John said.

"Not stumping for Grindell, are you?" Hood teased.

"No." Young John revealed the blue pamphlets with white letters. "These are yours. I was just doing some door to door."

"Where'd you get those?"

"Wally," Young John said, unable to mask his sheepish expression. "Some of us thought we could pitch in for your campaign. On our own time, of course."

"'Us?' Who's us?'"

"Me, Wally, Lester—a bunch of us deputies."

The sheriff suspected Otto was behind the recruitment

effort but decided to spare Young John from further questioning. Although his employees were volunteering on their own time, Hood worried their participation might create an appearance of impropriety. He resolved, however, to raise his concerns not with Young John, who was trying to be helpful, but with Otto. "Let me have those," he said.

Young John handed over the pamphlets, then said, "Something weird happened yesterday. As I was leaving the courthouse, some guy I've never met approached me about getting into recovery."

The abrupt change of topic prompted Hood to switch mental gears and refocus. Last fall, Young John's job performance had faltered, and he eventually admitted abusing alcohol. Although Hood never revealed his own addiction and recovery, he did help his deputy enter a treatment program. Young John completed the program but relapsed for a brief time in March before amassing the three months of continuous sobriety he now enjoyed.

"So this guy," Young John continued, "said his name was Tom and he was a friend of someone who was at the treatment center the same time I was. One of the things we're told is to help other people with recovery, so I asked Tom to join me on one of the benches outside the courthouse so we could chat. I was telling him about meetings around here and different groups—and everything seemed fine—but then he mentioned you."

"Me," Hood said, his surprise apparent.

"Yeah," Young John said. "He said something like: 'Do

you go to the same meetings as your boss?'"

"What'd you say?"

"I was, like, dumbfounded. I didn't know what to say, because you've never said anything about that. That's when I got suspicious and started asking him questions, but he was pretty evasive."

"Did he give you his name or the name of the person who was with you in treatment?" Hood asked.

"No. He said he wanted to respect his friend's anonymity. Then he tried to smooth things over by saying he only asked about you because his employer is also in recovery. He said if he and his employer attended the same meeting, it could be awkward."

Hood twisted his mouth into a puzzled frown.

"I didn't say anything," Young John continued. "I mean, I didn't know what he was talking about and, even if I did, I wouldn't talk about another person in the program. I decided just to cut the conversation short and we went our separate ways."

"Thanks," Hood said.

"I just thought you should know."

"I appreciate it." Hood started up the steps to the next house on the block.

"Where're you going?" Young John asked.

Hood held up the pamphlets. "I'm going to finish distributing these." What he didn't say was "and worry about what you just told me."

CHAPTER 12

"Sheriff Francis Hood to see Jay Bishop," Hood said to the receptionist at the newspaper's front desk.

He was directed to a short flight of stairs and told to turn left at the top and enter the frosted-glass door marked "Executive Office."

Once inside, he repeated his introduction to a woman seated at a desk in a reception area. Her name plate identified her as Veronica Snellen, Administrative Assistant. "Good morning, Sheriff. Jay will be right with you. Please have a seat." She gestured toward the unoccupied sofa, flanked by two chairs.

Hood surveyed the surroundings, which were neat, bright, and clean. If he had to choose a one-word description, it would be "smart." Veronica seemed to fit right in. She had intelligent eyes, her long, dark hair obviously was styled with precision, and her tasteful ensemble was well-fitted. Hood guessed she was in her mid-30s.

Before he sat, he shuffled through the orderly arrangement of magazines, all oriented toward news or finance. He purposely left the magazines in mild disarray before sitting down. The sheriff suspected Jay was employing the strategy of flaunting his executive position by keeping visitors waiting. Hood wondered whether he intentionally had mussed the periodicals, then scolded himself for his petty behavior, which he knew was incompatible with his recovery program's emphasis on humility. He was about to reorganize the magazines when the office door opened and Jay invited him in.

Jay directed Hood to one of three plush visitors' chairs before seating himself in a high-backed chair behind a massive, ornate mahogany desk. Hood noted the significant disparity in eye-level between the two men. He reminded himself to stop making assumptions.

"What can I do for you, Sheriff?" Jay asked.

"Did you write about the day your father disappeared, like I asked?"

Jay pressed a button on an intercom. "Ronnie. Do you have that thing I dictated for the sheriff?"

"Right here. Want me to bring it?"

"Please."

"On my way."

Jay had just released the button when a light tap on the door preceded Veronica's entrance. As she handed her boss the document, they exchanged wry smiles. Although Hood was unable to interpret the look, he sensed they were sharing an amusing secret.

Jay scanned the document, dismissed his assistant, and handed the paper to the sheriff.

Hood read:

"Up early. Diane slept in, so I made breakfast. Read Sunday paper while I ate. Then went to office to look over some new proposals. As usual, I lost track of time, but got to the house

> just before 1 p.m. Mom was fussing because Dad hadn't returned. Dinner was put on hold. George and I went to the site where he said he'd be. Found his car, but not him."

Hood turned over the page, which was blank on the back. "This is it?" he asked.

"That's it."

Hood removed a notepad and pen from his pocket. "Did you know in advance where your father planned to go that morning?"

"He may have mentioned it at work. I really don't remember. I do remember Mom telling us that morning that we should look for him at the development site, because that's where he said he was going."

"You said Diane slept in. Was your wife planning to drive separately to the family dinner?"

"No. She said she wouldn't be going. She wasn't getting along with my siblings at the time."

"All of them?"

"Anne, mostly. I think it was a woman thing. But she's not too fond of George, either."

"You went to the office that morning?"

"Yes."

"Is it typical for you to go in on a Sunday?"

Jay shrugged. "I wanted to get caught up. It's a family business. You work when you want to, you work when you need to, you work when you don't want to. It's whatever."

"What time did you get to the office?"

"I don't know—nine-thirty, ten."

"Was anyone else there? Did anyone see you?"

"Ah." Jay picked up a pen from the desktop and tapped it rhythmically on the blotter. "You mean, do I have an alibi? Did I see anyone at the office who can verify my story?"

"Did you?"

"No. I was alone." Jay stopped tapping and added, "The whole time."

"Which was, what, between two and three hours?"

Jay stroked his mustache. "You know, just because Mom recanted the family alibi, it doesn't mean one of us killed my father."

"I agree. But it does establish opportunity."

Jay smirked. "Growing up, I watched my share of cop shows on television. What was the slogan—means, motive, and opportunity, right? I hope you don't suspect the butler did it because we don't have a butler."

Hood let the sarcasm pass. He drew on a recovery program slogan—principles before personalities—and chose professionalism instead of antagonism.

"If you're looking for means," Jay continued, "it could be almost any one of us. Mother taught us how to shoot. She was quite the marksman—or is it markswoman? We're all quite handy with firearms—pistols and rifles. All except Henry, that is. Guns frightened him."

"I'm aware you and Anne won several junior titles," Hood said.

"It became quite the competition between us." Jay put

down the pen and leaned back in his chair. "Can you shoot, Sheriff? Are you a dead-eye?"

"I don't pull the trigger unless I'm sure I can hit what I'm aiming at."

"Good answer but let me give you some advice. Don't get into a shooting match with Annie. In addition to that quirky memory thing, she's an ace at repetitive motion activities. She took up golf one summer and she was a five handicap by autumn. Same swing, same contact, every time. She's like that with firearms, too. She beat me every time we competed. Used to piss me off. So, you know what I did?"

Hood shook his head.

"I stopped competing with her."

"I suppose that's one option."

"What about motive?" Jay asked. "Why would any of us want to kill my father? I'd say it would take a pretty strong motive to commit—what's the word for killing your father?—patricide."

Hood was developing some theories, but his purpose was to glean, not share, information. "I understand you supported a proposal to build a new printing facility."

"That's correct," Jay said.

Hood detected wariness in Jay's tone. "Was it your idea?"

"The newspaper industry is hemorrhaging." Jay said. "If we do nothing, we'll bleed to death. Newspapers will never be as timely as digital delivery. But that doesn't mean print is dead." As he spoke, he became more impassioned. "There are thousands of print publications that don't require immediate updates. They're niche-oriented weeklies and monthlies that cater to associations—farmers, auto dealers, you name it. If we build a state-of-the-art printing plant, we can compete for this business. The revenue would more than offset the costs of continuing the newspaper, which I would argue is a community service as well as a family tradition."

"But as I understand it," Hood said, "not everyone agrees."

"It's fear. It's what kills vision, innovation. Their business degrees tell them to calculate return on investment, and they freeze."

"I suspect the start-up costs are significant."

"Multi-millions," Jay said. "But there's also that long-standing business axiom that you've got to spend money to make money."

"Did your father support the idea?"

"Absolutely," Jay answered, without hesitation. "He was looking at a possible site when he disappeared."

"What about the other family members?"

"As usual, they were all over the place. Either they couldn't make a decision or they'd change their minds from one day to the next."

"How do you get along with your brothers and stepsister, not as family but as business partners?"

"If you're trying to psychoanalyze our—what's the word—family-slash-business dynamics, you may need to call in the professionals. A family business can be a volatile concoction. I'm inclined to think we're more dysfunctional than most families because we have more wealth, power, and possessions to fight over. What makes us comfortable also makes us covetous. Backbiting, building coalitions, and passive-aggressive behavior are the norm in the Bishop household."

Hood jotted the word *cynicism* in his notebook. "That really doesn't answer my question."

"Maybe I don't want to answer your question." Jay leaned back in his chair. "The point is, I don't need to answer it for you or for myself. As the eldest son, I was promised control, groomed for control, and now I have control. If the others want to skirmish and struggle with each other, it really doesn't concern me. I like to consider myself above the fray."

On his note pad, Hood wrote *arrogance* and underscored it. "I'd like permission to have a forensics team look over your Range Rover," he said.

"For what?"

"Evidence."

"Evidence of what?"

"Your father."

Jay leaned back in his chair and chuckled. "Of course you'll find evidence of my father. We drove together a lot." He resumed tapping the pen, this time against a cuff. "What exactly are you looking for?"

"A stain."

"Ah," Jay repeated. "Was it Anne or Henry who told you about it?" He stared at Hood momentarily, then added. "Never mind. It doesn't matter. Yes, you will find a stain of my father's blood from the time he cut his hand on a metal newspaper rack. I don't remember when it happened, but Anne will."

"May I have the keys?"

"Knock yourself out, Sheriff. Just be quick about it. Diane gets upset if I borrow her Escalade for too long."

"The keys?"

Jay activated the intercom. "Ronnie, would you give the keys to the Range Rover to the sheriff on his way out? Hold on," He released the button and asked Hood, "Are we about done?"

"For now," Hood said.

Jay pressed the button and said, "He's leaving now."

CHAPTER 13

"Where to next?" Hood asked his daughter, who was seated beside him in the family van.

Elizabeth consulted the list. "3112. Should be three or four houses up the block."

Hood smiled as he eased the van forward. He was delighted when his daughter suggested they spend the afternoon setting up yard signs. In addition, Otto had been elated when Hood called for a list of county residents willing to display "Re-elect Sheriff Hood" signs. As a bonus, the forecast called for a sunny day in the high 70s, a welcome departure from the intense heat and humidity of the past two weeks.

When he stopped, they got out and repeated the drill. Hood hefted the mallet from the cargo area and Elizabeth took one of the signs affixed to a wooden stake. They discussed the most visible location for the sign and Hood hammered the stake into the soil.

"Thanks for suggesting this," Hood said, as he laid the mallet in the hatch and closed the rear door.

"Sure."

Hood sensed she had no idea how much her presence meant to him. He had missed her during the more than ten months after his wife and daughter left because of his drinking.

He had expected to miss Linda but was surprised when he realized he missed Elizabeth as much, if not more.

He also was amazed he didn't harbor a resentment toward his wife for leaving. He realized, almost immediately, that it wasn't a choice for her, it was survival. His rationalization that he wasn't hurting anyone else had been the height of denial. Linda was in pain from watching the man she loved commit some bizarre form of slow-motion suicide. And Elizabeth had tried desperately to adapt to adolescence with a father who, despite being physically present, was mentally, emotionally, and spiritually absent.

Hood also was pleasantly surprised when Linda announced plans for her and Elizabeth to return home in early June. Although he had embraced recovery, he had expected the separation would last at least a year, if only because he had overheard Sarah counsel Linda to wait that long. Shortly after the move back home, Linda told her husband that Elizabeth's desire to reunite as a family was a major factor in the decision.

Hood climbed into the driver's seat and waited for his daughter to get settled.

"Turn right at the next intersection," Elizabeth said.

He didn't start the ignition. He simply looked at her, unable to mask his expression of delight.

"Do you want me to fasten my seat belt?" she asked, still consulting the list in her lap. "We're just going around the corner." When he didn't reply, she looked at him. "What?"

"I just want you to know how glad I am that you and your mom are back home."

"Yeah. Me too." Elizabeth said. "You know Mom's birthday is coming up. Do you know what you're going to get her?"

"She usually gives me a list of what she wants and I pick something from that."

"Her list is what she needs, not what she wants."

Instead of asking for clarification, Hood pondered the distinction. Elizabeth was right. Linda routinely listed practical items instead of personal gifts.

"What about taking her out to dinner?" Elizabeth suggested.

"You think she'd like that?"

"I think she'd love it. Take her to Derek's"

Derek's was widely acknowledged as the best restaurant in Huhman County, not that the competition was fierce. "Okay," Hood said. "Derek's it is."

They drove forward, repeated a sign placement, and returned to the van. "How's cheerleading practice?" Hood asked, referencing her summer challenge to learn the routines before classes resumed in the fall.

"Okay."

Hood sensed equivocation. "Just okay?" he prompted.

"It's a clique. The seniors think they're so great, the juniors are a bunch of posers sucking up to the seniors, and sophomores like Claire and me mostly sit on the bench, even though we work harder and perform better than a lot of the others."

"You'll get your turn."

"I know," Elizabeth said. "But if I do, I'll do things differently."

Hood thought of the line from the Serenity Prayer—*The*

courage to change the things I can. He started the van and pulled forward. "Different how?"

Elizabeth shrugged. "I don't know. Pick people based on their commitment to learn the routines, not just popularity."

"Sounds like a change for the better."

"If I stick with it, that is." Elizabeth pointed to a house on the right. "Should be this one here."

As they got out and repeated the routine, Hood asked, "You're not thinking about quitting the squad, are you?"

"You make it sound like I'm giving up or something," Elizabeth said as she retrieved a sign from the hatch. "It's just all so shallow."

"But you can change it," Hood said, trying to sound encouraging instead of argumentative. He grabbed the mallet. "Maybe not this year, but down the road."

"Maybe," Elizabeth said. She placed the stake in the lawn near the sidewalk. "Here okay?"

"Looks fine," Hood said.

"I've already decided to stay with it this year," Elizabeth said as her father tapped the sign twice, then drove it into the ground. "We'll see what happens after that."

Hood straightened and looked at the result of his labor.

"What do you think?" Elizabeth asked.

"I'm pleased."

"We've got plenty of time," Hood assured his wife as he turned onto Route DD, the site of Otto and Sarah Kampeter's annual barbecue.

Linda remained sullen. Although she had informed her husband, twice, of her desire to arrive early to help her sister with preparations, the father-daughter, campaign-sign chore lasted longer than intended. Hood explained, with apologies, that he had "lost track of time."

He didn't need his detective skills, however, to see she was miffed. As he slowed and steered along the Kampeters' gravel drive, the campaign signs—which weren't removed from the van in the ensuing rush—clattered as an annoying reminder of their tiff.

He parked beside a line of vehicles in a grassy area and, as soon as he pulled the emergency brake, Linda was out of the van. She opened the hatch and reached for a cooler filled with side dishes she had prepared.

"I'll get that," Hood offered.

"Fine." Linda walked hurriedly toward the house.

Hood and his daughter lingered by the van.

"Mom's pissed," Elizabeth said.

"Elizabeth." Hood intended a scold, but he smiled and added, "Yeah, she is."

As they unloaded the cooler and folding lawn chairs, Hood surveyed the activities already in progress. The Kampeters' small farm seemed designed to host a summer gathering. Groups of adults and children played volleyball, croquet, and horseshoes in designated areas. Some fathers baited hooks or demonstrated how to cast from the edge of a pond stocked with bass, bluegill, and crappie. Near a corral of indolent horses, Amy, one of the Kampeter nieces, used sugar cubes to coax a lone pony to suffer the indignity of a child rider while being led in a circle.

Hood and Elizabeth carried the chairs to what seemed to be the center of activity, the brick barbecue pit, where Otto's brother was manning the grill while gabbing and laughing with a group of male guests. They unfolded the chairs, adding to a cluster of vacant seats arranged under the shade of a massive oak tree.

"I'm gonna help Amy with the pony rides," Elizabeth announced as she hurried toward the corral.

Hood toted the cooler into the kitchen, where Linda already had donned an apron and joined the busy meal preparations. "Here's the cooler."

"Just set it down," she said.

He felt scolded, but not resentful. He knew punctuality and doing her part were important to her. "I'm sorry," he said.

"Thank you," she replied, indicating she appreciated the sincerely in his tone.

Although he remained penitent as he stepped outside, the apology had eased his mind. He was tempted to sit and enjoy a solitary moment, but he was eager to talk with Otto. He scanned the site and saw his brother-in-law assisting a young angler at the pond.

Hood headed in that direction, his progress interrupted as he greeted and shook hands with friends, family members, and acquaintances along the way.

Otto, who was kneeling and baiting a hook, noticed Hood's approach and stood. "Francis," he greeted.

"Otto, I need to talk to you. I ran into one of my deputies—"

"In a minute," Otto said. "First I want you to meet someone." He turned to a big man standing beside him. "Louis Doerhoff," he said to the man, "this is Sheriff Francis Hood, my brother-in-law and the incumbent in the Republican primary. Francis, this is Louis."

"Nice to meet you," Hood said. He extended his hand.

"My pleasure," Doerhoff said.

They exchanged a firm handshake.

"And this is my son, Danny," Doerhoff said. As Hood shook hands with the boy, his father added, "Otto's trying to show him how to catch a fish."

"Teach a man to fish," Hood said.

"I like that—a man who quotes the Bible," Doerhoff said.

Hood knew the origin of the quote was a topic of controversy but didn't correct Doerhoff.

"Now cast that line like I showed you and watch that bobber," Otto said to the boy. He turned back to the men and focused on Hood. "Louis is interested in helping your campaign, but he wanted to meet you before making a commitment."

"Of course," Hood said.

"From what I've seen," Doerhoff said, "you seem to be doing a good job, but this Grindell fellow seems to disagree. He contends you're soft on crime."

"Nonsense," Otto said.

"I do what's proved to be effective," Hood said, warming to a familiar topic. "Modern law enforcement has gathered a lot of statistics over the years and what we've found is the 'lock 'em up' approach can be counterproductive. It costs taxpayers a lot of money and doesn't effectively deter crime. The vast majority of the folks sitting in my jail committed a crime linked to drug or alcohol abuse. Reduce substance abuse and you reduce crime. That's why DWI courts and drug courts have been established. And they were established by lawmakers, not law enforcement. Why house a prisoner on the taxpayer's dime if the person can become a productive member of society? That's not just my approach, that's the collective—"

"Let me interrupt you for a second," Doerhoff said. "I understand the point of recovery and rehabilitation programs, but people want to be safe. They want to feel secure in their own homes or walking to their cars at night. Grindell claims his law-and-order agenda is what's needed."

"I understand that. When he says there are no victimless crimes, I agree. All victims suffer some degree of trauma. If the law-and-order approach eliminated crime, everyone would be on board, but let's be realistic; it doesn't."

Doerhoff folded his arms across his chest. "So what's your approach?"

"The two tools available to law-enforcement are prevention and punishment. Obviously, prevention is preferable, but we need to reach people while they're young, impressionable. Our agency focuses on youth by partnering with educators and community groups to provide school resource officers, character-building programs, and anti-drug education. Sadly, there's no way to measure how effective these programs are, but I believe they're making a difference."

"I keep hearing these so-called experts say kids who get into trouble aren't responsible for their actions. They blame parents, poverty, society, and all that. I think that's a lot of malarky. In my house, Danny knows he's responsible for his behavior."

"That's how I was raised and that's what I try to practice as a father," Hood said. "But I grew up in a two-parent home where Dad worked and Mom stayed home. They were married 46 years and we always had a roof over our head and food on the table, but that's not always the case—especially these days. One of my school resource officers knows a kid who cleans up his parents' bottles, beer cans, and vomit each morning, then gets his younger brothers and sisters ready for school and puts them on the bus before he heads there himself. Some kids have a lot on their plates these days."

"Grindell contends violent crime has gone up in Huhman County," Doerhoff said. "It was in his latest ad."

"I can answer that," Otto said. "I did some checking. In recent years, crime rates generally have been declining nationwide, in Missouri, and in Huhman County. However, a triple-homicide nearly four years ago was an anomaly that really skewed the math. Technically, the ad isn't wrong, but it sure is misleading."

Doerhoff turned to face the sheriff. "Anybody ever tell you you don't come across as a conservative Republican?" he asked, ending with a chortle that made the remark difficult for Hood to interpret.

Hood was tempted to say something about butting

heads with some members of the Republican Party Central Committee but didn't. Instead, he said, "I try to adhere to reason, not to labels used to identify political parties or liberal or conservative ideologies. My opponent seems to be playing to people's fears. I examine the evidence and follow what works. I like to think the voters will do that, too."

Danny noticed the gap in the conversation and said, "Dad, I'm hungry. Can we eat now?"

"Perfect timing," Otto said. "I see a line starting to form at the grill."

"Sure son," Doerhoff said. He put his arm around Danny's shoulder and added. "Sheriff, I'm glad we had a chance to meet. It's been an interesting conversation and, I must say, not what I expected." He turned to Otto and said, "I'll be in touch."

After the father and son walked away, Hood said to Otto, "I'm not sure if I helped the effort or not."

Otto shrugged. "At least he knows where you stand. Let's eat."

"In a minute," Hood said. He held up a finger. "Guess who I found distributing my pamphlets door to door?"

"A volunteer."

"One of my deputies," Hood said.

"One of your deputies who volunteered," Otto corrected.

"It doesn't look right," Hood said.

"Was your deputy in uniform?"

"No."

"So. What doesn't look right?" Otto asked. "If people volunteer to help on their own time, what's wrong with that?"

"I'm their boss. It could look like I pressured them to do it, or I might play favorites with the ones who are helping."

"Which is why I didn't tell you. I don't give you the name of every volunteer I recruit and I didn't tell you the names of the deputies who signed on. You can't play favorites if you don't know who they are."

"But the voters don't know that," Hood said.

"Look, Francis, I'm worried we're falling behind in this campaign. I talked to your chief deputy and he spread the word. These folks have stepped up. They're putting in a lot of hours, but if you have a problem with that, it's your campaign so it's your call."

Hood twisted his mouth into a crooked frown. He was undecided. He felt himself entangled in some variation of the political flip-flop. He had just told a prospective donor he was guided by reason, but in his argument with Otto, Hood cited appearances of impropriety while Otto provided solid rationale.

"You don't have to decide now," Otto said, putting a hand on Hood's shoulder. "C'mon. Let's eat."

CHAPTER 14

"Have you seen the morning paper yet?" Maggie asked her boss.

"No." Hood poured coffee into a disposable cup. "I usually browse through it here. Why?"

"There's an ad for the Grindell campaign. You're not going to like it."

"I'm sure of that," Hood said, his tone dismissive. "Anything big happen overnight?"

"Pretty quiet, based on the reports. They're on your desk, along with the newspaper."

"Okay," Hood said. "I'll take a look."

Hood walked unhurriedly to his office. Several reports were stacked beside the newspaper on his desktop. He routinely went through the reports first, but curiosity prompted him to open the morning edition. He leafed to page five, where a photograph hit him like a punch to the heart. The image depicted Hood, wearing his uniform and a Santa hat, smiling, drinking beer, and apparently groping a woman wearing an elf costume and sitting on his lap.

He recognized the photo immediately. It had been taken nearly two years ago at a county employees' Christmas party, held after business hours at The Hideaway, a local bar and restaurant. The young woman was Cheri Ott, who had worked in the circuit clerk's office. Hood had been trying to move the tipsy elf from his lap, which led to an awkward entanglement. What Hood didn't know was who had taken the picture or how the Grindell camp had acquired it.

The caption below the photo read:

Is this the example you want your sheriff to set?
Party time is over.
Elect a sheriff who is committed
to protecting your family and your property.
Vote for Steve Grindell, Republican for sheriff.

Hood scanned to the small print at the bottom of the ad and read: Advertisement paid for by Citizens for Community Betterment. Joe Miller, treasurer.

Hood was livid. His hands shook as he fumbled his cell phone from his pocket and called Otto.

"Good morning, Francis," Otto answered.

"Is it?" Hood asked, an angry challenge. "Have you seen Grindell's ad in the morning paper?"

"Hold on."

Hood waited impatiently while Otto retrieved the edition.

"It's obviously a dark money ad," Otto said.

Hood was surprised and miffed by the nonchalance in his brother-in-law's tone. "We need to do something," he said. "Is that even legal? Can they use my picture without my permission?"

"Take a breath, Francis."

Hood was further exasperated by Otto's calm counsel, but he inhaled a long breath.

"I've never heard of the Citizens for Community Betterment or this Joe Miller fellow," Otto said. "Have you?"

"No."

"Got to be dark money," Otto concluded.

"But Grindell said from the beginning he wasn't going to go negative. We agreed to that."

"Grindell may not have known anything about this. That's the rationale for a dark money advertisement. The candidate can distance himself from it. It's worked so effectively at the national and state levels, local campaign managers are adopting it. They establish or find a group with a name that appeals to voters, find a straw man to serve as treasurer, and operate a sniper campaign separate and apart from the candidate's more positive approach."

"Couldn't Grindell put a stop to it?"

"He can ask, but not demand. He could threaten to withdraw as a candidate, but why would he? Negative campaigning works. Voters are hypocrites. They say they hate negative campaigning, but they pay attention to it."

Silence dominated the telephone connection, creating an unbearable heaviness for Hood. "What are we going to do?" he said, finally.

"Let me think about it," Otto said. "But my initial thought is to do nothing."

"I think I need to respond. I need to defend myself and explain—"

"When you're defending and explaining, you're losing," Otto reminded. "Think about that."

"All right," Hood said, his resignation apparent.

After they disconnected, Hood carried his nearly empty cup back to the coffee machine. He lifted the pot, glanced at Maggie's cup on the dispatcher's desk, and asked, "Need a warmer?"

"Sure." As he poured, she said, "I'm surprised Grindell would stoop to something like that."

"Me too. I called Otto and he said it's probably a dark money ad. He said Grindell may not even have been aware of it."

"That happens," Maggie said. "Would you be okay with me looking into it—on my own time and using my own computer?"

Hood returned to the counter and refilled his own cup. "I don't want you to go to any trouble."

"That wasn't the question," Maggie said. "I know how you feel about using department time or resources for the campaign, and I agree. Do you mind if I look into it on my time?"

Hood replaced the pot on the burner. "You really don't have to—"

"I know I don't have to. All I'm asking for is your permission."

"I guess," Hood said.

"Thank you."

THE FORGET-ME-KNOT

* * * * *

Hood parked in the lower lot at the St. Gotthard Tribune and watched the bundles of newspapers travel along the conveyor system. The track extended from an open overhead door to an area in the parking lot where carriers hefted the bundles and loaded their vehicles for delivery.

Hood reminded himself once more to practice open-mindedness in his scheduled meeting with George Bishop. He switched off the ignition, opened the door, and heard the commotion—a vehement argument between George and another man.

"You've gotta get your shit together, George," the man shouted. "This is the third week you've been late. I know you think this is just some Podunk county weekly, but I've got stores and rural customers who are counting on me. When you're late, I'm late, and people get pissed at me."

"They get pissed at me, too," George countered. "Don't think my phone doesn't ring."

"But I'm the one who suffers. If I don't finish my route and get to my second job on time, they're gonna can me."

"Not my problem. I've got enough on my plate with outdated equipment and congested distribution. Look around. We can barely get a semi in here to deliver newsprint, let alone have room for all these carriers' vehicles. How many times—?"

"Whoa, whoa," Hood said as stepped between the two men. "Let's bring it down a notch?"

"All I'm saying," the man said, "is some things need to change."

"We're working on it, okay. We're looking for a site for a new printing plant, somewhere near a highway, not in the middle of downtown."

"I've been hearing that for months, George. It's getting old."

"Well, it's the best I can do. You know and I know these are tough times and a project like this costs lots of money."

"All I know is talk is cheap," the man said. He turned and walked to his vehicle.

"What was that all about?" Hood asked.

"Press broke down—again. Sterling County weekly is late—again. He's pissed—again. All in a day's work. What do you want?"

"We have an appointment."

"Shit. Was that today?"

"Yes," Hood said. His voice was firm.

"Just when I thought this day couldn't get any worse." George assessed the delivery process, which seemed to be going smoothly. "All right. Come on."

Hood followed George through the distribution area, past the press room and into a claustrophobic, cluttered office a hoarder would envy.

"There's chairs behind you," George said. "Grab one."

Hood lifted one of the white, molded plastic chairs from a stack in the corner and set it in front of what was visible of George's desk. "Did you write the narrative I asked for?" he inquired as George stepped between cardboard boxes and over a stack of bound manuals to get to his desk chair.

"What narrative?" George asked.

"About what you did the morning your father disappeared."

"I don't remember being asked to do that. Besides, I don't have time for busy work."

Hood thought if George had ever joined the military, a drill instructor's first order would be, "Wipe that smirk off your face, private." George's manner and his facial expression—canted brows, narrowed eyes, smug grin—projected annoyance and arrogance.

"A death investigation is hardly busy work," Hood said, his chiding tone intentional.

"Fine. Can I just tell you?"

"I guess." Hood removed his pad and pen from his uniform pocket.

"We work late Saturday night. Deadline's midnight to put out the Sunday morning paper. As always, I closed up about one in the morning, grabbed a copy of the paper, and headed for that 24-hour truck stop out where the highways intersect. I had me some bacon, eggs, hash browns, biscuits and gravy while I read the sports section, then headed home. I was in bed by three, slept till 10:30 or 11, showered and went to my parents' house."

"You're divorced, correct?" Hood asked.

"What's that got to do with anything?"

"Just trying to establish if you interacted with anyone from the time you got up Sunday morning until the time you arrived at your parent's house."

"Nope."

"And what time did you get to their house?"

"Around noon. I try to get there a little early. Sometimes I get to spend some quiet time with Mom before everyone gathers and the weekly battles begin."

"Tell me about the battles."

"It's a family matter. We're related and, back then, we were all part of my father's business. It made for some interesting discussion is all I'm saying,"

The Bishop family dynamic was precisely what Hood was trying to understand. He was pre-empted from any follow up, however, when George abruptly changed the subject with his question, "Have you seen Grindell's campaign finance reports?"

"I have."

"So you know I'm his biggest donor?"

"Yes," Hood said.

"Then you can understand why I'm reluctant to say too much to you."

"Just say what's on your mind," Hood said, his exasperation evident.

"I'm not sure I'm going to get a fair shake from you."

"Because you're backing my opponent."

"And because I've made no secret of the fact that I think you botched the first investigation of my father's disappearance."

"This is nothing personal. I'm approaching this investigation—"

"I don't think that's possible. You respect my mom, I can tell. You like Anne. You think she's smart, which she is. But you don't like Jay or me—or Julian, for that matter."

Hood suddenly felt transparent. He had been trying to maintain objectivity, but George's comment was right on point. Hood had been playing favorites. He knew he needed to get honest with himself and reconsider his approach. "I'm trying to keep an open mind," he said. "Did you notice anything different about anyone's behavior around the time of your father's disappearance?"

"Different how?"

"Anyone seem anxious, preoccupied?"

"Henry was a mess, but I found out later it was that job offer in Florida."

"Anyone else?"

"No. Not really," George said. "Say, can I ask you a question?"

"Sure. Go ahead."

"The other day when you had us gather at the house, Julian said something to you about being in Iowa that morning. What did he mean by that?"

"What people say to me during the course of an investigation is confidential," Hood said. "I wouldn't, for example, tell—"

"He wasn't in Iowa that morning," George said.

"What do you mean?" Hood was dumbfounded. Doubt had been cast on the alibi Julian and Kim had offered—the alibi he had verified and accepted for nearly a year.

"When I was at the diner, I saw his truck," George said. "He came off the Highway 43 ramp and headed into town on 50 East."

"You're certain it was Julian's truck?"

"Absolutely. It's one of a kind. He patched or primed the fenders since then, but it was his truck, all right."

"Was Julian driving?"

"That I couldn't see."

"And this was what time?"

George shrugged. "I was just watching out the window waiting for my order to come up, so I'd say around 1:30 in the morning, maybe closer to two.

"Have you mentioned this to anyone else?"

"After Anne walked you out and came back, I asked her if she knew what Julian was talking about."

"Okay," Hood said, "but I'd appreciate it if you didn't mention it to anyone else. This is new information for me. I'll need some time to look into it."

"Whatever," George said. "Look, I'd better get back out there and make sure those morons don't get those bundles mixed up."

Hood welcomed an end to the interview. He had new information he was eager to investigate.

As he drove eastbound on Highway 50—out of his jurisdiction and into neighboring Sterling County—he pondered whether George had been truthful about seeing Julian's truck on the morning of James Bishop's disappearance. If true, it provided opportunity for Julian—and/or Kim—to be involved in the disappearance.

He turned onto Route E and headed northbound.

In his experience, investigations were about separating truth from lies, facts from assumptions. With regard to physical evidence, he relied on experts—including Loeffelman the medical examiner and Sandra from the crime lab—to make determinations. With eyewitness accounts, however, it was up to him to determine truth and accuracy. Essentially, it was a question of trust.

He steered into the gravel parking lot of Checkered Flag Auto Service, which also housed Ed McCullough Racing, Inc. All five overhead doors were closed.

Who do I trust? he asked himself as he parked, got out, and rapped on the single standard door. *Who can I trust?*

He peered through the pane of glass in the door. He saw no activity, heard no footsteps approaching. He took out his cell phone, scrolled to the number he had saved for Julian, and called.

"Hello," Julian answered.

"This is Sheriff Francis Hood. I'm at Checkered Flag, but no one seems to be around."

"We're on the road, Sheriff—about 100 miles from Rossburg, Ohio. Racing at Eldora Speedway tonight."

"I need to speak with you."

"Go ahead. I've got nearly two hours to kill."

"Not on the phone. In person. When will you be back?"

"Late Monday, I'm guessing."

"Can we meet Tuesday?"

"I guess."

"Okay. I'll call you Monday night to work out the details."

CHAPTER 15

Hood heard the gunshots.

They sounded in rapid succession, in bursts of four. He walked from the parking area, crested the berm, and looked into a large natural amphitheater carved into the soil and surrounded by embankments of earth, shrubs, and saplings. On the arena floor, a lone shooter stood at the firing line, aimed at a target about ten meters distant, and fired another cluster of four shots. From his vantage point, Hood watched the projectiles shred the black bullseye.

The shooter ejected the magazine and holstered the handgun under her arm. She turned and removed her ear protection as she walked to a picnic table positioned well behind the firing line.

"Nice shooting," Hood called out.

Anne squinted into the early-afternoon sun. "Sheriff," she said, after a moment of recognition. "How long have you been watching me?"

"Just got here." Hood scampered down the berm and joined her at the picnic table.

"Did you come here to shoot?" she asked.

"No," Hood said. "I come on Wednesday evenings when the range is reserved for law enforcement."

"I wondered why it was closed then. Now I know." She appraised the sidearm holstered on the sheriff's hip. "How about a friendly competition? Your Glock nine against my H and K forty-five."

Hood chuffed. "I don't know if my ego could take it."

"What do you mean?"

"Your brother warned me."

"Which one?"

"Jay."

"What'd he say, exactly?" Anne reloaded the magazine.

"He said 'don't get into a shooting match with Annie.' He called you Annie, by the way."

"I know. He only does it to antagonize."

"He also said when he realized he couldn't beat you, he just stopped competing."

"When did you talk to him?"

"A couple days ago—at the newspaper."

Anne pushed the magazine into the firearm until locked into place. "Did you meet Ronnie?" she asked, emphasizing the name.

"His receptionist?"

"Jay calls her his administrative assistant. I think she came up with the title."

Hood was curious about the change of topic. "Yes. Why?"

"Just asking."

Hood heard the pique in Anne's tone. "Something I should know about?"

"Why not? Everyone else does. They flirt with each other

like adolescents. I don't know if they're actually having an affair, but it's embarrassing to see them together. And Jay's got a good thing with Diane. I'd hate to see him muck it up."

Hood recalled Jay's comment about "a woman thing" dividing his wife and sister. "How do you get along with Diane?"

"Fine." Anne walked to the firing line, replaced her noise reduction earmuffs, and resumed her shooter's position.

Hood was mesmerized by her movements as she drew her handgun, leveled it smoothly, and squeezed four shots into the bullseye. She switched the weapon to her non-dominant left hand and repeated the firing sequence, with one bullet slightly wide of its mark. Then she knelt and put another four bullets into the target's center.

She holstered the gun, removed the earmuffs, and returned to the picnic table.

"Impressive," Hood said.

"Thanks."

As she repeated the reloading process, Hood asked, "Do you recall seeing a stain in the hatch of Jay's Range Rover?"

"I'm surprised Jay volunteered that."

Hood sidestepped her observation and said, "He volunteered it was a blood stain from when your father cut himself on a newspaper rack. Were you aware of that?"

"Yes. That was his explanation when Henry and I both noticed the stain."

"When and where did it happen?"

"I wasn't there when Father cut himself."

"No. I mean when you noticed the stain."

"Oh, that was July 21, nearly a year ago. We were at my parents' house, after the Sunday meal, and Henry and I were helping Jay load some boxes Mother had packed."

"What was in the boxes?"

"Stuff from Jay's childhood. When he moved out, he left a bunch of stuff in his bedroom. Mother got tired of asking him to remove it, so she boxed it up herself and asked Henry and I to help Jay load it."

"Before the time you noticed the stain, do you remember your father wearing a bandage on his hand?"

Anne hesitated before answering and closed her eyes, almost as if watching a replay. "No. Come to think of it, I don't."

"But you would remember, right?"

"If I saw him wearing it, but I wasn't around him every day. Is this part of the investigation?"

"As a rule, I don't discuss the investigation."

"But you just told me you met with Jay and what you talked about."

"I needed to hear what you observed. There are exceptions to the rule."

"I could probably help your investigation, you know, if you're willing to confide in me, that is. And not just because of my memory."

Hood said nothing.

"You still think of me as a suspect, don't you?" Anne asked.

"It has nothing to do with you. What you're proposing would be inappropriate under any circumstances."

"Have you talked to Henry yet? Can you at least tell me that?"

"I did. He sent me his recollections by email, and I followed up with a phone conversation."

"But you won't tell me what he said—about going out walking, I mean?"

"No."

"Have you talked to George?"

"Yesterday. We had an interesting conversation."

"Oh," she said.

Hood couldn't decide if her monosyllable indicated surprise or curiosity. "Normally, I wouldn't share what your brother told me, but he said he mentioned it to you after I left your parents' house."

"About Julian's truck?"

"Yes. He said he saw Julian's pickup here in Huhman County early on the morning your father disappeared. If he's telling the truth, Julian's alibi is worthless."

"What did Julian say about it?"

"I haven't talked to him yet. He's on the road, due back Monday."

"Have you talked to Kim? Don't forget she was with him."

"No, but I will."

"When you do, just remember Julian broke up with her after she got pretty heavy into drugs. It was a bad breakup. I wouldn't trust anything she says."

"I'll keep that in mind," Hood said.

* * * * *

As Julian tightened the intake manifold on the sprint car's motor, he glanced at the second-place trophy he had won at Eldora Speedway in Rossburg, Ohio.

"What're you thinking?" Rusty asked. Monday mornings were reserved for repairing and tuning the race car after the weekend campaigning. For both mechanics, the enjoyment of working on the sprint car far exceeded diagnosing "funny" sounds or changing the oil in minivans or SUVs.

"It was decent purse and a nice trophy, but—" Julian said, allowing the remainder of the sentence to evaporate.

"You're not the first driver and you won't be the last to suck on Stevie's exhaust. There's no shame in second at Eldora."

"Still sucks," Julian said, deflecting the compliment as his cell phone's ring tone sounded. He straightened, looked at the caller identification, and answered, "Hello, Sis." He continued to use the term of endearment for Anne although years had passed since he'd lived in the Bishop household as her foster brother.

"Hey. Did I catch you at a bad time?"

"It's okay." He handed the torque wrench to Rusty and walked to a corner of the spacious interior of the single-story garage and workshop. "What's up?"

"You left Mother's house the other day before I got a chance to talk to you. What did you think of the sheriff's visit?"

"I don't really think about the sheriff much."

Anne wasn't certain of his meaning. "The reason I'm

calling is I talked to the sheriff this weekend."

"Yeah. He called me while we were on the road. Said he'd call back today to set up a meeting."

"That's why I wanted to give you a heads-up. He knows your alibi is bogus."

"What do you mean? You were the one who suggested I should have an alibi. You said your mom had come up with one for you guys, and I should have one for me and Kim. That's the whole reason I made up the story about staying overnight in Iowa."

"I know," Anne said. "I'm sorry about that, but after Mother gave us an alibi, I thought you should have one, too."

"So what happened?"

"You mentioned the Iowa alibi to the sheriff when we were all gathered at Mother's house. One of my brothers heard you and told the sheriff it couldn't be true because he saw your truck early on the morning Father disappeared."

"Which brother?"

"Doesn't matter. What matters is the sheriff will be asking you about it. I'm sure that's why he wants to meet with you."

"So what should I do?"

"I don't know," Anne said, her frustration apparent. "I just didn't want you to get blindsided. You better let Kim know, too. It's better if you two are on the same page."

"We don't really see each other anymore. She's kinda pissed at me."

"Do you think she'd try to get back at you by telling the sheriff you lied about the alibi?"

"I have no idea what she'd do. I've heard she already moved in with some other guy—some drug dealer—and she's pretty strung out all the time."

"Yeah, I heard that, too," Anne said, "but maybe that's good. I told the sheriff not to believe a word she says."

"Good. Look, sis, I gotta go. I'll talk to you soon. Okay?"

"Okay," Anne said.

CHAPTER 16

Sterling County, population 13,568, read the sign Hood passed as he drove eastbound on Highway 50.

He glanced at the dashboard clock and calculated he would arrive on time for his 10 a.m. appointment with Julian at Checkered Flag Auto Service.

As he turned onto Route E, his cell phone rang. He activated the hands-free option in his cruiser and answered, "This is your sheriff."

"Glad I caught you, Sheriff," Julian said. "I either got some bad food or a stomach bug, but I had to leave work. I won't be able to meet today."

"I'm already in Sterling County," Hood said. "Can I just stop by your house?"

"No. I've been throwing up all morning. I don't want you to get what I've got. Can we talk another time?"

"Hold on a minute," the sheriff said. As he pulled his cruiser to the shoulder and stopped, he considered the possibility that Julian was feigning illness. He also considered attempting to interview Julian by phone right now. Despite his reluctance to postpone the conversation, he said, "When?"

"Soon as I'm better," Julian answered. "Can I call you, like, tomorrow?"

"All right. I'll be expecting your call."

After they disconnected, Hood called his Sterling County counterpart, Sheriff Dennis Schaeperkoetter.

He requested and received the address for Julian's former girlfriend, Kim Green, as well as directions. He also was informed the residence was the property of her current boyfriend, who was being held in the Sterling County Jail while awaiting trial for drug distribution.

Hood stepped on the splintered wooden pallet—which served double duty as welcome mat and mud scraper—and rapped on the battered screened door.

No answer.

He knocked again and heard a garbled sound he translated as "Who is it?"

"It's Huhman County Sheriff Francis Hood. I was hoping to have a word with you." He scanned the makeshift shelter, a bizarre blend of dilapidated trailer and tumbledown shack. The muddy yard was strewn with clumps of knee-high weeds, assorted auto parts, and the remains of an El Camino resting on cinderblocks instead of tires.

He heard another muffled, unintelligible phrase from within.

"Hello," Hood called. He peeked through a triangular hole where a corner of the screen had come loose and folded upon itself. Inside, a woman was splayed on a tattered sofa. Her denim shorts were ripped just below the buttocks and her crop top revealed a fragment of a large tattoo on the small of her back.

"Go 'way."

"Kim, I just need to talk to you for a few minutes."

"Oh, for fuck's sake."

Hood heard her movements and her approaching barefooted steps. He stepped back to avoid being hit when she pushed open the screen door. The young woman who stood before him was a cadaverous version of her former self.

When he first interviewed Kim nearly a year ago, she was bright-eyed, energetic, and attractive. The woman he faced had been transformed into an emaciated, strung-out zombie with a sallow complexion and matted hair. She stared at him with hollow, vacant eyes.

Hood was no stranger to the signs of meth addiction. In his line of work, he had seen it often, and each time, it left him with scar tissue.

"I came here to talk with you about Julian—"

"We're not together anymore."

"I'm aware of that. When we talked last August after the disappearance of James Bishop, you told me you and Julian spent the night together in his camper after a race in Iowa."

"So?"

"So I have new information that shows it isn't true. A witness saw Julian's truck at the highway intersection in Huhman County early that Sunday morning."

"Who said that?"

"A witness."

She shrugged. "Yeah, well I really don't remember."

"Because," Hood said, "since you and Julian were together back then, I could see how you might have felt—"

"You saying I lied?"

"No. I'm just saying you might have felt pressured—"

"What's in it for me?" she asked abruptly.

"I don't understand."

Kim jutted her chin forward, as if preparing a challenge. "C'mon, Sheriff. You want me to rat out Julian, say we weren't together, what do I get out of it?"

"That's not what this is about."

"Sure it is," she said, her voice becoming louder. "I see you looking down your nose at me, how I'm looking, where I'm living. You think I'm so jacked up, I don't know a shakedown when I see one?"

Hood carefully stepped back off the pallet and into the mud. He realized he had made a mistake coming here unaccompanied and confronting a substance abuser. He also understood how even an unimpaired person might misconstrue his comments as some kind of bribe or quid pro quo. He decided to return another time.

"I'm sorry," Hood said. "I shouldn't have come."

"Damn straight."

As he began to turn away, a new thought intruded. He faced Kim and said, "This is probably none of my business either. But there's a recovery program offered by Huhman County Hospital. It's called New Opportunities. I've—"

"Not interested," she said.

"Okay." As Hood walked to his cruiser, he heard the screen door slam behind him.

"God . . ."

Hood joined the chorus of voices.

". . . grant me the serenity to accept the things I cannot change, the courage to change the things I can, and the wisdom to know the difference."

Matthew surveyed the diverse group of people who had gathered for the weekly meeting of Recovery Rules. "We open every meeting by reciting the Serenity Prayer," he said, "and there's a reason for that. The first line of the prayer talks about acceptance, but what does acceptance mean for you? Who wants to start?"

"I'm Francis, alcoholic," Hood said, surprised by the sound of his voice. He hadn't intended to speak but felt compelled to share.

When the greetings subsided, he continued. "How do you accept not being able to help someone get what you've got?" He looked at the wall, avoiding eye contact. "I mean, today I was talking with this young woman I hadn't seen in almost a year, and I couldn't believe it. She used to be an attractive girl, but she started doing meth and now she looks like an extra in a horror movie.

"It's so frustrating. I told her about the hospital's recovery program. I was going to give her one of the brochures I keep in my cruiser, but you know what she said? She said, 'not interested.'"

The room was dominated by absolute silence—no throat clearing, no sipping from coffee mugs, no scraping of chair legs.

Hood scanned the faces of the people seated around the table. "'Not interested.' How do you accept that? How do you just walk away and not feel helpless? Because, right now, I've got to tell you, I'm feeling pretty helpless." Hood turned to the man seated beside him. "I'll pass to Mac."

"Mac, alcoholic," the man said, followed by the customary collection of greetings.

"I appreciate what you shared, Francis, and I appreciate your honesty. I've been there. I stopped drinking and my life got better. The program asks me to pass it on, to help others receive the gift that was so freely given to me. So when people reject it outright or try but can't seem to hold onto it, it's a disappointment. But I can't internalize that disappointment and frustration, and I certainly can't drink over it. My role is to share my story and what I've learned. I can't change someone else, but I can help if that person wants to change. As one of our slogans says, 'I can't make God's miracle.'"

Hood lingered after the meeting concluded, which was not unusual. He often used the time to converse privately with Matthew while they cleaned up after the meeting.

"Sounds like you had a rough day," Matthew said.

"Yeah, and it's too bad because I've been feeling pretty good about myself lately."

"Why's that?"

"I faced a challenge the other day and was tempted to drink over it, but I didn't," Hood said.

"Tell me about it."

"Well, as the incumbent sheriff, I expected the endorsement from the county Republican committee to be a sure thing. Turns out I was wrong." Hood saw the change in his sponsor's expression and added, "I know what you're going to say—expectations are resentments waiting to happen."

Matthew said nothing.

"But, here's the thing," Hood continued. "I appeared before the committee and I had a resentment going in, even before they started quizzing me. They grilled me pretty good, and I think I sounded pretty annoyed by some of the questions. When it was over, I was feeling like I may have cost myself the endorsement and I pulled into a convenience store."

Hood saw the change in Matthew's expression—lips twisted, eyebrows up.

"I needed gas," Hood said, defensively. "But," he conceded, "next thing I know, I'm sitting in my car staring through the window at the liquor aisle and thinking about how a drink would take the edge off." He deliberately paused and sipped coffee. When the silence teetered on awkward, he added, "But I didn't drink. I thought it through and I drove home." He drained the remainder of his coffee. "So what do you think?"

"Did you consider calling me?" Matthew asked.

"I thought about it. I know something similar happened last fall and I called you then, and you helped me get through it. But this time I was able to do it on my own. That's good, right?"

"How were you able to do it on your own?"

"I'm not sure I understand the question."

"Do you think it was your own will power or did you seek guidance?" Matthew asked.

"Well, I didn't call you, so will power, I guess."

"When you were drinking, was your will power enough for you to quit?"

"No. I tried, but couldn't. That's when I knew I needed help."

"And you asked for help?"

"Yes."

"But now you believe your will power kept you from drinking?"

Hood saw himself in a quagmire of contradictory behavior even before Matthew finished the question. "Okay," he said. "I see what you're getting at."

"This isn't a reprimand," Matthew said. "It's a caution. I've done it myself. I think I've turned something over to my higher power and then find myself trying to take it back. Even as a kid, I remember saying, 'I can do it myself,' whenever help was offered. I believed asking for assistance was a sign of weakness. So I grew up relying on independence, individuality, and sheer will. When it came to addiction, however, I learned my will power was not enough."

Thoughts collided in Hood's mind. He expected a pat on the back, not a blow to his ego.

"Consider this," Matthew added. "Your defense against drinking wasn't your will, it was recovery, including the reminder, the slogan, to think before you drink."

"Okay," Hood said, his tone contrite.

They resumed cleaning up, working silently side by side until Hood said, "There's something else I wanted to talk to you about."

"Go ahead."

Hood related what Young John had said about being approached by the stranger, Tom, who inquired about Young John's stint in rehab, then asked the deputy if he attended recovery meetings with his boss. "Thing is," Hood added, "I don't think Young John knows I'm in recovery. He seemed pretty surprised by the question."

"How did your deputy reply to this Tom fellow?"

"He didn't know what to say. He said he tried to get more information, but the guy clammed up."

"Do you suspect Tom has an ulterior motive?" Matthew rinsed the coffee pot and set it in the drying rack.

"I don't want to be paranoid, but I've already seen some negative campaigning backed by dark money. I think Steve Grindell is a stand-up guy, but his campaign manager, Chip Luther, is a hired gun from St. Louis who used some nasty tactics to unseat the state auditor. And Luther is being paid by George Bishop, who'd like nothing more than to unseat me."

"But breaking anonymity and outing an alcoholic? That's about as low as a person can stoop."

"I can see the ad slogan now," Hood said, "'Elect Steve Grindell. He's not a drunk.'"

Matthew removed the damp coffee filter and grounds,

then dropped them in the trash. "How can I help?"

"I could use some advice. Do you think I should stop coming to meetings, at least until the primary is over?"

"What do you think?"

Hood had become accustomed to Matthew's habit of tossing a question back to him. He didn't like it, but it wasn't unexpected. "I don't know. The meetings give me something tangible. When I listen to others share their alcoholism and recovery, it's more than just slogan and concepts, or even words. It's something real I can hold onto."

"What do you think would happen if you stopped?"

"I think it would be like anything else, like exercise, for example. If you lose momentum, your fitness suffers."

"Are you in a position where you can afford to lose momentum, knowing your recovery will suffer?" Matthew asked.

"You mean: Will I relapse?"

"If it were me," Matthew said. "I would need to ask myself if I was risking a relapse and, if so, if it's worth it?"

Hood thought for a moment, then said, "You know, you have this maddening tendency to answer a question with another question."

"This is your decision, Francis. I can't make it for you. All I can do is share the questions I would ask myself before acting."

Hood was satisfied he had received all the counsel Matthew was willing to give, but dismayed because he felt no closer to making a decision. "I'll think about it," he said.

CHAPTER 17

Although Hood knew self-pity could drag him under, he found himself wallowing in it. And the more he tried to extricate himself, the more mired he became.

His investigation of James Bishop's disappearance was leading nowhere—again. Julian hadn't called Tuesday as arranged. Moreover, Julian appeared to be avoiding him—not answering or returning his calls. Hood had contacted Checkered Flag Auto Service on separate occasions and reached Ed McCullough or Rusty Koenigsfeld, but both men said Julian had continued to call in sick.

Hood also believed his reelection bid was floundering. Grindell was out-spending and out-hustling him, what had become known as the Christmas Party ad continued to unnerve him, and he feared his alcoholism might become a campaign issue.

In addition, the temptation to drink was more intense than it had been in months. *Just one*, a voice in his head nattered relentlessly.

He walked to the firing line where he previously had watched Anne practice; his goal was to match or beat her display of marksmanship. He pulled his 9 mm. Glock from its holster, leveled it and fired four consecutive shots into the target's bullseye. He crouched and repeated the sequence with the same results.

"Nice shooting," Young John called from where he stood some twenty feet away reloading his service weapon.

"Thanks." Hood stood and fired another burst of four bullets. One strayed wide of the mark.

He ejected the magazine, inhaled a deep breath, and holstered his weapon. As he walked to the picnic table, he heard the gunshot and the sound of a bullet whizzing between him and Young John as it chipped up gravel and ricocheted into the berm.

Hood froze for a split second before his mind signaled alarm. "Take cover," he shouted.

Young John hit the ground as Hood instinctively crouched and ran toward his deputy. He put himself between Young John and the direction of the gunshot and pulled his deputy behind the picnic table—the only available cover.

Hood snatched his ammo box from atop the picnic table, then tipped the table onto its side to provide a better shield.

"You okay?" Hood asked, as he reloaded.

"Yeah," John said. "What the hell?"

Hood peeked between the table slats and focused on the wooded hilltop where he believed the shot had originated. He saw no movement.

"Hey," he yelled.

He heard no response, saw no activity.

"Cease fire," he shouted. "People are here on the range."

No reply.

"You think it was an accident?" Young John asked, his voice shaky with uncertainty.

"Maybe," Hood said, "but it's a risk I'm not willing to take." He took his cell phone from his pocket, called Maggie, and explained the situation.

Hood disconnected and settled in to wait. Although his intuition suggested the shooter was long gone, his senses remained on heightened alert. He watched the movements of every squirrel, heard the chorus of songbirds, and felt the gentle touch of each breeze.

"It's kind of serene out here when there's not a lot of guns going off," Young John said.

The serenity was short-lived. Within minutes, blaring sirens sounded, sheriff's cruisers spewed dust and gravel, and deputies fanned out in all directions, scouring berms and hillsides for a shooter who had disappeared.

Hood's gut roiled.

He opened the refrigerator and considered his options—iced tea, chilled water, a soft drink. None appealed to him.

Thoughts bombarded his brain.

The incident at the gun range had left him shaken. A part of him fixated on explanations. He wanted to believe the gunshot was an accident, but—as the medical examiner so often reminded him—he had no facts. Wally had insisted on searching and using a metal detector to scour the hillside for a shell casing or other evidence, so Hood took some solace that a clue might be found.

Another part of him focused on the case. The initial investigation collapsed because everyone had an alibi. Now, no one did.

In addition, he was anxious about the upcoming candidate forum. Public speaking was not his forte, and the event would be broadcast countywide on the local public access channel.

The refrigerator's chime sounded, scolding him for leaving the door open too long.

"Are you okay?" Linda asked.

"Yes," he lied. He closed the door.

"Isn't it about time to leave for your meeting?"

"I'm going to skip tonight."

She came closer and put a hand on his shoulder. "Are you sure?"

"I just need a break."

"Okay."

He heard the disappointment in her voice. He wanted to explain his reasons, to justify his decision, to be honest with her. But he couldn't. Not now.

"You're right," he said. He forced a smile, took his keys, and drove from the house.

He knew he had left Linda with the impression that he had changed his mind, but he had no intention of attending the meeting.

He had no idea where he was going.

He drove, seemingly without direction, until the lighted sign for Good Times Liquor Store came into view. The sign beckoned. As he slowed to turn into the parking lot, he realized he had not been driving aimlessly; he intended to come here. At the last possible moment, he accelerated and passed the entrance to the liquor store.

Not tonight, he told himself.

He didn't slow again until he rounded a bend and watched in his rearview mirror as the sign diminished, then vanished.

He continued driving until he found himself on Schoolhouse Road, where he turned onto the gravel road—no longer guarded by a deputy—that led to the Trestle. The parking area overlooking Cooper Creek was vacant. He walked to where the command post had been dismantled and sat on a rough bench someone had crafted from a downed tree trunk.

The Trestle was no longer an active crime scene. The remains of James Bishop had been removed, the evidence—scant and seemingly insignificant—had been collected, and the sheriff's department's presence withdrawn.

The scene, like his investigation, was dormant.

The question—*Who do you trust?*—echoed in his brain. *Who was lying or, at least, not telling the whole truth?*

Honesty had been the topic at a recent recovery meeting. Since then, he had thought about it quite a bit. And he realized he hadn't been disclosing the whole truth, at least not to his wife.

He hadn't told Linda that he narrowly escaped being shot—accidentally or intentionally—at the gun range.

He hadn't confided in her about his fears that his alcoholism might be revealed publicly in an attempt to derail his re-election.

And he hadn't mentioned that Anne recently had greeted him with a kiss on the cheek. He had wondered what that was about. In high school, he had never approached Anne, had never seriously considered it. High school was a popularity-based caste system, and Anne's popularity level was multiple tiers above his own. Within the system, any attempt to advance came with a risk of rejection and humiliation.

Now, nearly thirty years later, Anne not only was friendly, but also treated him warmly.

Was she flirting?

Hood wasn't certain. What he knew, if he was being honest—there was that word again—was his ego had been inflated. Attractive, intelligent Anne Bishop—the girl with a one-in-a-billion memory—was paying attention to him.

He was flattered.

He believed he would never cheat on Linda. He never had seriously considered the possibility. But he hadn't mentioned Anne's behavior to his wife, either. He wondered why.

In many ways, he still was trying to reestablish his relationship with Linda after their separation. Or, perhaps, he was attempting to create a new relationship by bringing a different self to the partnership. As an alcoholic, he was controlling, intolerant, and closed-minded. He expected other people to follow his directions and, if they didn't, he was resentful.

In recovery, he was encouraged to be humble, tolerant, and open-minded. He was reminded to accept what he couldn't change.

He felt he was making progress—as a person, husband, father, friend—but he still had a long way to go. A measure of progress would come when he was able to be entirely honest with Linda. He had told himself he didn't want to disturb and upset her, but he wondered if he was, again, merely justifying keeping secrets.

Headlights on the gravel road pulled him from his thoughts. A pickup truck appeared and stopped in the lot. Two teenage boys emerged from the truck and began unloading fishing tackle.

"Sheriff, is that you?" asked the taller of the two.

Hood recognized him as his Wally's eldest son, Luke. "It sure is, Luke."

"Hey, I hope this is okay," Luke said, lifting his tackle box. "Dad said you cleared the scene and we could fish here."

"Go right ahead," Hood said. He arose from the makeshift bench and walked toward his vehicle. "Fishing for catfish?"

"You bet," Luke said.

"Well, good luck."

"Thanks."

Hood started the ignition and headed for home.

CHAPTER 18

The courtroom seemed an appropriate setting for the personal trial Hood was enduring.

He sat stiffly in the witness box and listened as the debate moderator—perched in the judge's high-backed chair between and above the two candidates—made introductory remarks. To the moderator's left, challenger Steve Grindell occupied the chair normally reserved for the court stenographer.

Hood felt himself perspiring in the harsh glare of the lights set up by the television camera crew as the moderator outlined the format for the first of two scheduled debates. Following opening statements, the candidates would face questions from a trio of local reporters—representing print, radio, and television—seated at the prosecutor's table. In the center and a side aisle were the TV cameras operated by volunteers from the local public access channel, which was airing the debate.

"We'll begin with incumbent Sheriff Francis Hood," the moderator said, prompting a cue from the camera operator nearest to the sheriff.

Although Hood had rehearsed his three-minute opening statement ad nauseam, anxiety produced an unanticipated stammer in his voice. His goal was not to botch his opening statement, but he felt himself teetering on the brink of panic. He purposely slowed his speech and attempted to steady his delivery. By some seeming miracle, he settled into a confident rhythm. When he finished, he felt relieved and satisfied.

Although Hood assumed he was temporarily off camera, he feigned attentiveness as Grindell described his 22-year tenure with the St. Gotthard Police Department and his rise through the ranks—from officer, to lieutenant, to captain. He used the remainder of his time, as Hood had expected, espousing a hard line on crime.

"Our first question," the moderator announced, "is from KGBW reporter Samantha Meyer and goes to Sheriff Hood."

Hood attempted to quell the adrenalin-fueled tremor coursing through him.

"Sheriff," the reporter began, "some law enforcement officers contend drug and alcohol abuse plays a role in up to ninety percent of criminal behavior. How would you characterize the county's drug problem, what steps have you taken to combat it, and what additional actions can the public expect if you're re-elected?"

"Thank you for that excellent question," Hood said, applying Linda's advice to be courteous and complimentary. "I don't know the exact percentage, but I wouldn't dispute that number. With regard to the problem, we've taken and I plan to continue a multi—" He paused, searching for the elusive word. "I plan to approach the problem from a variety of ways. I mean, in lots of ways from a variety of approaches."

He reminded himself to breathe and paused to inhale a

steadying breath. "When it comes to drugs—and this is true of most crimes—we need to consider both enforcement and prevention. We have laws on drug dealing and selling and possession, and we need to enforce those. And we do. But we also need to work on prevention."

He sensed his words tumbling and stumbling over each other in a rush of release. "I mean, it's like supply and demand. We need to address supply—enforce the law and cut off supply—but we also need to work on lowering demand. That's where prevention efforts are important. We've got drug courts to try to decrease repeat offenses. We've got D.A.R.E—that's Drug Awareness Resistance Education—in the schools. We've got to continue to hit the drug problem from all sides."

He stopped, setting off a chain reaction of colliding thoughts as he tried unsuccessfully to replay a mental recording of what he had said and evaluate if it made sense.

"Captain Grindell," he heard the moderator say.

"That's all well and good, what the sheriff just said," Grindell began, "but let's keep our proper roles in mind. We appoint judges to run the courts, we rely on parents to rear their children, we hire teachers to help educate them, and we elect a sheriff to enforce the law. As a sheriff, that's what I'll do. I won't try to be a judge or a teacher or parent or even a social worker, for that matter." He paused. "My job will be to enforce the law. That's what the people elect a sheriff to do."

Grindell seemed to inflate, as if energized by the momentum of his own words. "These drug dealers are scum.

They sell drugs to our kids and get them hooked and pocket the cash—and lots of it. The dealers get rich and the kids get hooked or busted, maybe for possession or maybe for stealing money, even from their parents. Well, I'm here to tell you: When I'm elected sheriff, those days are over. I'll bring every resource I can muster to root out the dealers and put them where they belong—behind bars."

Hood felt warmth flush his face with the realization that Grindell had staggered him with a law-and-order haymaker. He barely heard the next question—something about juvenile offenders—or listened to Grindell's response while he crafted a damage-control explanation.

"Your views, Sheriff?" the moderator said when Grindell had finished.

"If I may," Hood began, "I'd like to follow up on my previous answer and my challenger's response. I understand we all have roles to play and the sheriff's job is to enforce the law. And I do. The Huhman County Jail is near capacity, but I'm not proud of that because each offender translates into at least one victim and significant costs to taxpayers. A crime that is prevented, however, leaves no such carnage or consequences. The reason crime prevention doesn't enjoy the same mass appeal as law-and-order rhetoric is because prevention can't be shown on a chart. I can tell you how many offenses are reported and how many people are in the jail, but I can't tell you the number of crimes our department has prevented. I can't prove a negative, and I'm beginning to doubt that I can successfully campaign on one. But I believe prevention efforts are concepts whose time has come. Prevention spares victims and saves money, which benefits everybody. Which brings me to juvenile offenders."

Hood's comments on the juvenile issue were abbreviated and incomplete, due to time limits. The debate's multitasking—speaking, listening, concentrating, reevaluating—frustrated him. He recalled Otto's axiom of politics—"when you're defending, you're losing"—and reminded himself to stay in the moment.

"Our next question," the moderator said, "comes from *Tribune* reporter Robert Wadkins."

"Sheriff," Wadkins said, "our newspaper recently published an advertisement from the Citizens for Community Betterment group that showed you at a Christmas party wearing a Santa hat and consuming what appeared to be an alcoholic beverage while a younger woman sat on your lap. So far, I have heard no comment, explanation, or rebuttal from you regarding the ad."

Hood was annoyed, but not surprised, the issue had reappeared. "Is that a question?"

"The question," Wadkins said, "Is would you like to respond to the ad?"

Despite his reluctance, Hood felt trapped. "Okay, I'll address this one time, and hopefully that will be the end of it. Some workers at the courthouse arrange an annual Christmas party for county employees. It's held after business hours in a private room at a local restaurant. They take up a collection to rent the room and buy gifts. No county funds are involved. I've played Santa for the last couple of years. Yes, I recall drinking one or two beers and, yes, one of the workers sat in my lap for, like, a few seconds while I was distributing gifts. I know the photo looks like some drunken orgy, but I can assure you it was nothing like that. It was a harmless gathering of co-workers."

Before Wadkins could pose a question to Grindell, the challenger said, "I'd just like people to know I had nothing to do with that ad."

"But, Capt. Grindell," Wadkins said, "did you make any effort to stop the ad from publication?"

"How could I stop it?" Grindell answered, his indignation apparent. "I didn't know about it. I don't even know who the Citizens for Community Betterment are." He faced the sheriff. "Look, I have the highest regard for Sheriff Hood. We agreed from the beginning this wouldn't be a negative campaign. I was as appalled to see the ad as he was."

Hood knew he'd been set up and knocked down. The dark-money, white-hat combination was brilliant and clever. The political action committee had launched a negative attack, setting the stage for an outraged rebuke from the candidate occupying the moral high ground.

Grindell may not have known about it, Hood thought, but he certainly had taken advantage of it. He wanted to cry foul, to lash out.

But, mostly, he wanted to be somewhere else. Anywhere else.

CHAPTER 19

"You're in early," Hood said as he entered the department and joined Maggie, who was at the counter filling her mug with coffee.

"I came in hoping I could talk with you for a few minutes before I get started," she said, gesturing toward Amber, who was finishing her overnight shift at the dispatcher's station.

"I came in early, too," Hood said, "so it's your lucky day. But in my case, I couldn't sleep after my debate debacle last night."

"You're too hard on yourself," Maggie insisted. "You were fine."

She extended the coffee pot. Hood separated a disposable cup from the stack on the counter, and Maggie filled it.

"Let's go to the break room," Hood said.

Maggie lifted a laptop and several pages of printed notes and followed her boss. They settled in molded plastic chairs on opposite sides of an eight-foot, rectangular table. Maggie placed her notes and laptop on the table.

"I wanted to bring you up to speed on what I found out about the Citizens for Community Betterment," Maggie said. "It should only take a few minutes."

Hood nodded.

"The group is registered with the IRS and Missouri Department of Revenue as a 501(c)(4), a tax-exempt, non-profit organization. I know about 501(c)(3) designations because two of the charities I work with are C-3s, but I had to research C-4s."

"What's the difference?" Hood asked.

"They're similar, but not the same. C-4 is the designation for a social welfare agency. As such, it must spend a majority of donations to promote the common welfare or general good or however it's phrased, but it also may spend up to 49.9 percent of its contributions on political campaigns, either for or against a candidate." She lifted the lid of the laptop. "But here's the wrinkle—they're not required to disclose the names of their donors."

"So," Hood said, "we don't know and can't find out who financed the Christmas Party ad?"

"Exactly."

"But if the group is tax-exempt, it must be accountable somehow."

"It is," Maggie said. "Federal and state regulations to establish a C-4 are complicated, but the bottom line is three trustees must be named, officers must be elected, and the records and reports are open to the public."

"Except the names of donors?"

"Correct," Maggie repeated. "But I was able to get the names of the trustees, who also serve as the officers."

"Anyone we know?"

"No one I know," she said. She slid one of the pages across

the desk. "But here's a printout. Any of these names ring a bell?"

Hood scrutinized the names and offices—Nancy Werdehausen, president; Constance "Connie" Bax, secretary; Joe Miller, treasurer. None was familiar. He reread them, then looked up. "No."

"Me neither. So I went on social media and searched for them. Have you finally gotten on social media, Francis?"

"My daughter set up a password and profile for me, but I don't use it much. I don't really have time for that."

"It can be a time-saving resource," Maggie said. "But I've got to be careful not to get sucked in. If I get distracted and start going down rabbit holes and exploring links, I can get lost for hours. It's like an addiction." She realized the implications of the word the moment she said it and pressed her fingers to her lips.

Hood smiled. "Might not be the best thing for me, given my history," he said. "So, what did you find?"

"I'm still working on it. I'm not 'friends' with any of them, so biographical and other information is limited. I could send friend requests to them, but I haven't. Since the group paid for the campaign ad against you, I was worried the trustees might be suspicious if they received a friend request from someone who works for the sheriff's department."

"Good thinking."

Hood heard the unmistakable sound of the computer powering on, followed by the click of keystrokes.

"But here's what I did find out. Joe, the treasurer, is a graduate of Josef Gottfried Catholic High School and Rockhurst

University in Kansas City. He's a retired Missouri Restaurant Association executive. I couldn't find Connie, the secretary, so I'm assuming she doesn't have a presence on social media. Nancy is a 1991 graduate of R-1 high school. She also—"

"That's my graduating class," Hood said.

"You're right," Maggie said. "I forgot. Anyway, she graduated from the University of Missouri in Columbia and its medical school. She's an OB/GYN at Huhman County Hospital. The social media site said she and I have a mutual friend, Susan Schulte, who is an administrator at the hospital.

"How do you know her?"

"We both serve on the hospital's Partners group, which helps recruit and retain volunteers.

"I don't think I know her."

"Probably not," Maggie replied. "Why don't you ask your wife if she knows Susan since they both work at the hospital?"

Hood shrugged. "Sure."

"And while we're at it," she said, sliding the laptop across the tabletop, "why don't you log on to your profile and see if you share mutual friends with those officers?"

"Now?"

Maggie glanced at the clock; she had twelve minutes before her shift started. "You're right," she said, her tone apologetic. "I probably should relieve Amber."

"Actually," Hood said, "the truth is I don't remember my password. I don't use it much, so I tried to have just one, but every time I'm asked to create a new one, it asks for more letters, or upper and lower case, or numbers, or characters like an exclamation point or dollar sign. It's maddening."

"It's designed to enhance security."

"Well," Hood said, clearly aggravated, "I ended up writing my passwords on a sheet of paper that sits next to my computer. How secure is that?"

"Okay," Maggie said, "but will you at least try it when you get home?"

"Sure," Hood said.

"Found it," Wally said, his excitement apparent as he stood in the open doorway of his boss's office.

Hood couldn't help but notice his chief deputy's sweat-soaked underarms and collar, and the brown, triangular burrs known as sticktights clinging to his pant legs.

"Found what?" Hood asked.

"A cartridge casing. I found it on the hillside at the gun range where you thought the bullet came from."

"Where is it?"

"It's at the crime lab. It's obviously from a rifle, but ballistics will be able to identify caliber and stuff, plus whether there's any fingerprints on it."

Hood knew a spent cartridge without a weapon would be of limited value, but he didn't want to dampen Wally's enthusiasm. "Good work," he said. "Thanks for taking time to do that."

"Sure," Wally said. "By the way, I watched the debate last night. Good job."

"Thanks," Hood said. "Have you got a few minutes right now?"

"Sure," Wally repeated. He settled into one of three visitors' chairs. "Is this about the incident at the gun range or the debate?"

"Neither," Hood said. "I'm trying to keep my mind off both right now. I'm trying to focus on the Bishop investigation, but I think I've hit a wall."

"I know the feeling," Wally said. "Sometimes, everything seems to fall in place. Other times, it's like prying away stones after a rockslide."

"I'm prying, but nothing's coming loose."

"Have you heard from the lab about the blood in Jay's—what was it—Range Rover?"

"Sandra said the amount was small. If it came from a bleeding corpse, it had to be wrapped pretty well. She said Jay's explanation that his father cut himself unloading a metal rack would be impossible to disprove."

"What about Henry taking a walk that morning?"

"He has a plausible explanation. He was in a quandary about a job offer."

"You said George saw Julian's truck that morning. What does Julian say about that?"

"I haven't—" he began, his answer interrupted by the sound of his desk phone ringing. "Hold on," he said to Wally. He picked up the receiver, punched a button, and said, "Yes, Maggie."

"Sorry to interrupt, but I thought you'd want to know. Anne Bishop is here. She'd like to see you."

Hood covered the mouthpiece, whispered "Anne" to Wally, then told Maggie he'd be right out.

After he disconnected, both men stood.

"I'll be next door," Wally said.

"We'll continue this another time," Hood followed his deputy out the door. As Wally disappeared into his office, Hood intercepted Anne and escorted her to his.

"Are you all right?" she asked.

Hood heard concern in her question. "I'm fine," he said. "Come in."

Hood opted to sit in one of the visitor's chairs. When a conversation was not official business, he preferred parity. Anne sat beside him in a similar chair, leaving a vacant chair on the end instead of between them.

"I was so worried," she said. "When I heard you'd been shot at, I—"

"Where did you hear that?"

"At the gun club. It's all the talk. Squad cars racing in, officers in riot gear with shields, helmets and tactical weapons fanning out across the grounds. They said you were pinned down behind a picnic table and—"

"Stories have a way of getting embellished."

"Francis, don't downplay what happened."

"I have to accept that I make enemies. It comes with the job. I arrest people, they suffer consequences, they become vindictive." Hood chose his next comment carefully and purposely. "Sometimes, even an investigation can provoke retaliation."

Anne shook her head. "How can you be so dismissive?"

"It was probably an accident," Hood said, although he was certain it wasn't. "I mean, I was at a gun range. Shots get fired."

"People who visit gun ranges know basic safety. They're not likely to do something stupid. If they did, we'd have accidents all the time."

"Well, I know you, your mother, and the rest of the family know their way around firearms, but not everyone is that competent."

"You may be giving some of my stepbrothers more credit than they deserve."

"Oh?" Hood said, hoping his monosyllable would elicit specifics.

"You already know Henry hates guns. George can be a little, what's the word, unpredictable, especially if he's been drinking and especially with handguns."

"When your family was involved in competitions, was it mostly rifles, handguns, or both?"

"Depends, Mother and I competed mostly with handguns. The boys did both because they also hunted."

"Except Henry."

"Yes," Anne replied. "George doesn't hunt much either. Jay and Julian are the hunters. Jay's got a pretty nice collection of guns. He typically goes on at least one out-of-state hunting trip each year."

A brief silence ensued until Anne asked, "Can we change the subject?"

"Yes."

"It's a personal question."

Hood was tempted to decline, but he knew questions sometimes revealed as much as answers. "Go ahead," he said.

"Are you in recovery because of a drinking problem?"

The question rocked him. He tried to remain impassive. "Where did you hear that?"

"I don't remember."

"*You* don't remember?"

"Okay, I overheard George asking Jay if he knew anything about you being in recovery."

"What did Jay say?"

"He said he didn't know. I figured since people were asking about you, I'd go to the source and ask you directly."

"I appreciate that." Hood instinctively crossed his arms and his legs. He had been careful to protect his anonymity. Matthew's group was the only meeting he attended, and he was careful not to reveal his surname, but he suspected some members recognized him as sheriff. He knew recovery programs were intended to be confidential, but confidentiality extended only as far as the biggest blabbermouth. "That's kind of a personal question," he added.

"I know," Anne said. "That's why I asked if I could ask a personal question."

When he didn't reply, she continued, "You don't have to answer. It's okay. I just thought you should know some people out there have been speculating about that and the separation from your wife."

"Jesus," Hood said, more loudly than he intended. "Why

are people so interested in my private life?"

Anne reached out and patted his knee.

Instinctively, Hood pushed his chair sideways, away from her touch, prompting Anne to withdraw her hand.

"Because you're a public figure," she said. "You're the sheriff and this is an election year."

"So why can't they talk about my job performance, public safety, that sort of thing? Why this emphasis on my personal life?"

"Because it makes for great gossip. It may sound ironic, but people like trying to resolve the seeming paradox between your private life and public persona.

"By people, you mean George?"

"He's not the only one."

"You, too?"

"I'm not proud to admit it, but yes, Francis. Me, too."

Hood glanced at his wall clock. "Well, I appreciate your concern—about the shooting and all—but, if you'll excuse me, I have to leave for an appointment."

Anne's expression indicated she detected a lie.

"No, really," Hood said. "It's at one o'clock."

"With who?"

"Well, if you must know for me to retain any credibility, it's with Jay's wife, Diane."

As Anne arose from her chair, she muttered—loudly enough for Hood to hear—"I don't envy you that conversation."

CHAPTER 20

"You realize, Sheriff," Diane said, "if a customer comes in, I'll need to break away."

"Of course," Hood said. He surveyed the collection of original art—including paintings and pottery, hand-crafted jewelry, and antique furniture.

"This boutique," Diane continued, "is a one-person operation, so I'm management and labor, including balancing the books, stocking the shelves, and dust-mopping the floor."

Hood looked at the hardwood planks—not a dust bunny to be found.

"Let's sit at the bistro table," Diane said, gesturing toward a small, round, wrought-iron table flanked by two matching chairs.

The chair appeared tiny and uncomfortable, a suspicion confirmed when he sat.

"Do you like tea, Sheriff?" Diane asked.

"Sure," Hood lied.

"Are you married, Sheriff?" she asked, as she busied herself at a counter behind the register.

Hood was caught off guard by the question. "Yes," he answered.

"What's her name?"

"Linda." Hood felt uncomfortable, perhaps because he had anticipated asking questions, not answering them.

"Do you have an anniversary coming up?"

"We were married in May," Hood answered.

"Too bad. That bistro set would make a wonderful gift. You two could enjoy lovely autumn evenings sipping wine on your patio or deck."

Hood pinched the tag hanging from the table and glanced at the price—$500. He decided not to mention Linda's birthday was today.

Diane approached carrying a tray with a floral teapot, two matching cups and saucers, and matching sugar and cream containers. She was dressed stylishly in black slacks, black stacked-heel sandals, and a black top featuring tiny geometric shapes in primary colors. She filled the cups, set one before the sheriff, and said, "This tea service is also for sale if you're interested, but it's rather pricey."

Hood, who was about to lift the cup to his lips, stopped and said, "Now I'm a little nervous."

"Don't be silly," she said. "If I use it and break it, I buy it."

"What if I break it?"

She shrugged, offering no clue of the consequences.

"Well, thanks for taking time to see me," Hood said, relieved to move beyond the small talk and sales pitches. "I know you weren't at Jay's parents' house on the day his father disappeared, but did you get a chance to write what you did that day?"

"Yes, but I don't see why it's important."

"It's my experience that things which may seem trivial by themselves take on greater importance as more information is collected."

"Like grains of sand in a mandala."

Hood visualized the artistic, intricate patterns in circles of sand. "Yes," he said.

"I'm impressed. Are you an artist, Sheriff?" she asked, as she handed him a printed page.

"Only an admirer," he said. "May I take a moment to read this?"

"Of course."

Hood read her narrative, which was as comprehensive as it was bland. Diane had slept late, made herself what she referred to as "presentable," and enjoyed a light breakfast. She drank two cups of tea while reading the Sunday newspaper, then immersed herself in finishing a novel, which she described as a cozy mystery.

Hood folded and tucked the page into his pocket. "I noticed you didn't mention any engagements or appointments. Did you see or talk with anyone else that morning?"

"No."

"Did you have a reason for skipping the Sunday dinner that day?"

"Not really. Sometimes I go with Jay, sometimes I don't." She tested her tea in a manner as dainty as her cup. "At some point, we stopped making excuses and his family stopped asking."

Hood was reminded of times when, as an alcoholic, he

would skip family gatherings because they interfered with his drinking. "Was there a reason you didn't attend regularly?"

"Not really," she repeated. She sipped again; her expression revealed satisfaction. "That's not true. The truth is I never really felt like I belonged. Maybe that was my fault, but none of them ever said or did anything to make me feel, you know, like I was part of the family."

"Any one in particular?"

"Not really."

The phrase seemed her default answer. "I was given to understand there might have been some friction between you and Anne."

Diane straightened. "Who said that?"

"I'd rather not—"

"I'll bet it was my husband. He thinks no two women can get along for two minutes without getting into some kind of cat fight."

"So you and Anne—"

"It's his secretary—excuse me, administrative assistant—I'd like to sink my claws into. The way she manipulates him."

"Veronica?"

"Call me Ronnie," Diane said, mimicking the voice. "She's got Jay so wrapped around her little finger. I wish he could see himself. It's pathetic, really."

The remark triggered a litany of complaints from Diane about her husband's behavior. Hood attempted, without success, to steer the conversation back on track, finally giving up when a bell above the door sounded, signaling a customer's arrival.

"Excuse me, Sheriff," Diane said, as she arose.

"Of course." He moved his chair carefully away from the table and stood. "Thanks for your time, but I really should get going."

"But," Diane said, glancing at his nearly full cup, "you haven't finished your tea."

"Another time, perhaps."

Finally, Hood thought, as he steered into the gravel lot at Checkered Flag Auto Service and parked behind Julian's truck.

During previous visits, announced and unannounced, either the business was closed or Julian was absent. He walked to the open garage bay door and waited for the deafening sound to subside.

Inside, Julian sat in the sprint car, pressing and releasing the accelerator, while Rusty Koenigsfeld stooped over the open engine compartment and adjusted the throttle.

Rusty looked at Julian and made a throat-slitting gesture, signaling he was satisfied.

Julian cut the motor, restoring silence, and climbed out of the cockpit.

"Julian," Hood hollered, his voice echoing in the cavernous garage.

"Sheriff," Julian said, his surprise apparent.

"I need to ask you some questions," Hood said.

Julian hesitated, then replied, "Now's not a good time."

Hood advanced into the interior. "Make time."

"Okay," Rusty said, intervening. "I'm gonna leave you guys to it and get some lunch. Want me to bring you anything?"

Julian—apparently resigned to facing Hood's questions—requested a double cheeseburger with large fries. Hood shook his head, even though he wasn't sure if the offer included him.

"To drink?" Rusty asked Julian.

"I'll grab a beer from the fridge."

As Rusty left, Julian walked to an aged refrigerator and pulled on the grease-stained handle. He retrieved a beer and offered one to the sheriff, who waved it away. Julian perched on one of two stools beside the workbench and motioned Hood toward the other.

"So," Julian asked, twisting the cap from the green bottle. "What's this about?"

"Can you tell me where you were on Wednesday, between say five and seven p.m.?"

"This past Wednesday?"

Hood nodded.

"Home. Probably having a TV dinner and watching reruns of old sitcoms. That's what I usually do about that time on weekdays."

"Did anybody stop by? Anybody who could verify you were home?"

"Do I have an alibi, you mean?"

"Yes."

"Why?" Julian asked. "What happened?"

"Somebody took a shot at me while I was at the gun range."

"Yeah. Anne told me about that, but she didn't say when it happened." Julian swigged beer. "What makes you think it was me?"

"I'm just asking."

"Well, it wasn't."

"Okay. Different topic. What would you say if I told you somebody saw your truck in town the morning James Bishop disappeared?"

"Who?"

"A witness."

"I'd say your witness needs to get their eyes checked."

"You're sticking with the alibi you were in Iowa?"

Julian stared out the open bay door and took a long pull on his beer. "Could have been a truck that looked like mine. Did your witness see me driving?"

"I'm not going to disclose the extent of my information."

Julian swiveled on his stool. "I'll take that as a no."

Hood sensed Julian was buying time before answering. In his experience, people who were telling the truth didn't do that. Stalling was a liar's tactic. "I talked to Kim the other day," he said.

"So it was Kim?" Julian's voice was louder, angrier. "We're not together anymore, you know, and she's plenty pissed at me. She'd say anything to get back at me." He faced Hood. "Look, she was jonesing pretty bad that night, so we did end up driving back. But it had nothing to do with James Bishop's disappearance. I was so tired when we got home, I crashed big time, but I gave Kim the keys to my truck so she could find her dealer and get a fix."

The revelation hit Hood like a one-two punch: first, the admission the alibi was a lie; second, Julian's willingness to implicate Kim.

Hood sensed the Julian who stood before him now was not the same person he questioned the previous August. Former Julian appeared torn; he was infatuated with Kim but realized he might need to leave her because he couldn't save her from her addiction. But now, Julian seemed intent on vilifying the woman he couldn't live with or without.

"Just so you know," Hood said, "Kim didn't tell me anything."

"But you said you talked to her."

"I did, but I did most of the talking. She pretty much told me to get lost."

"So she didn't say anything about us coming back that night?"

"Not a word."

"Look, all I can tell you is I had nothing to do with the old man's murder. I have no idea what Kim was up to. Maybe she was hitting him up for money. All I know is she had an expensive habit she couldn't afford."

Hood said nothing. He knew he would need to follow up on Julian's suggestion that money might have motivated Kim to approach James Bishop. And, depending on what he learned, he anticipated he would have more questions for Julian.

"Just so we're clear," Hood said. "I don't like wasting the county's tax dollars trying to track you down because you won't answer my calls. I want your word that it won't happen again."

Julian nodded.

"Good," Hood said. "Enjoy your lunch."

Hood exited his cruiser and surveyed his surroundings.

If anything, the near-perfect conditions—bright sunshine, robin's-egg blue sky, verdant backdrop—provided greater contrast to the dilapidated hovel where Kim lived.

Hood stepped onto the wooden pallet and rapped on the wooden screen door.

No answer.

"Kim," he called.

No response.

"It's Huhman County Sheriff Francis Hood. I talked to Julian."

Nothing.

Hood peeked through the triangular hole in the corner of the screen and saw the lower portion of Kim's body sprawled on the floor.

"Kim," he shouted, as he pulled on the latched door. It bowed but held.

He yanked more forcefully and the latch sprang free. He rushed to her, knelt, and checked her vital signs. Her breaths were shallow, her pulse weak.

He called 9-1-1.

* * * * *

Hood was familiar with the emergency room waiting area at Huhman County Hospital. At one time or another, he had sat, paced, read, slept, sipped coffee—which was surprisingly good—or waited impatiently for information.

He remembered awaiting an update—on varying occasions—about his wife, daughter, in-law, friend, deputy, victim, even a convicted felon. As best he could recall, however, this was the first time he awaited a report on a suspect.

The realization that Kim was a suspect rattled Hood. During his time in recovery, he had learned addiction is nondiscriminatory. And he had embraced the notion that addicts in recovery aren't bad people trying to become good, they're sick people trying to get well. He recalled the wasted time and unrealized potential during the time he was shackled to the bottle.

Although Hood didn't pray much, he silently appealed for her to live, not only so she could answer his questions, but also in hopes she would seek long-term recovery. He asked that she find what he had found.

The sound of a door opening interrupted his entreaty, and he stood when a doctor appeared in the otherwise empty waiting area.

"Sheriff Hood?" He phrased it as a question although he obviously recognized the uniform. "I'm Doctor Randall."

"How is she?" Hood asked.

"She's stable. She's asleep right now. We'll need to run

some additional tests once she's awake and alert."

"Overdose?" Hood asked.

"Yes. Toxicology detected a synthetic amphetamine, likely meth. It's a good thing you found her. You may have saved—"

"Can I see her?"

"As I said, she's asleep. She's unable—"

"I'm not going to question her. I only want to see her—just for a minute."

"Very well."

The doctor escorted Hood to the room, where he waited by the door while Hood stood by the bed and silently recited the prayer commonly used at his meetings. "God, grant me the serenity to accept the things I cannot change, the courage to change the things I can, and the wisdom to know the difference."

CHAPTER 21

Hood was straightening the papers on his desk, in preparation for the end of another workday, when Wally appeared in his doorway.

"On your way out?" Wally asked.

Hood focused on what Wally was holding—a clear plastic bag containing a spent bullet cartridge.

"I'm in no hurry," Hood said, his curiosity piqued.

Wally placed the bag with the bullet casing on his boss's desk. "Ever heard of a 5.56-millimeter NATO cartridge?" Wally asked. He sat in one of the facing chairs.

"Isn't that military ammo?"

"Mostly," Wally affirmed. "You'll find that cartridge used in some of the weapons developed by the U.S. Armed Forces and NATO allies. That's where the name comes from. And guess what else?"

"What?" Hood said, automatically.

"That's what some of the snipers in Iraq and Afghanistan used."

"And you found this on the hillside at the gun range?" Hood asked.

"Right around where you thought the shot came from." Wally said. "I believe that's from your bullet."

Hood didn't share Wally's certainty. Bullet casings, he reasoned, abound at gun ranges. Shooters pick them up to reload, kids pocket them as souvenirs, and nothing proved the casing had contained the bullet fired in Hood's direction. Nevertheless, the casing was found in an area where weapons were not permitted to be discharged.

"There're no prints on it," Wally added. "Not even partials. I'm guessing the shooter was wearing shooter's gloves."

A military rifle and shooter's gloves, Hood thought, pointed to the probability that the shooter was a serious marksman, a speculation Wally voiced when he added, "You know what I think? I think whoever shot at you knows more than a little about guns."

Hood nodded. "If that's true—and it seems likely—the key question is was it an accident, a poor shot, or an intentional miss by an excellent marksman."

"What do you figure the distance was? Seventy-five yards?" Wally asked.

"More like a hundred."

"I can go back out there and walk it off, but—either way—I don't see any decent shooter missing from that range with a sniper rifle."

"So, intentional then."

"I'm guessing someone wanted to get your attention."

"Why leave the cartridge behind?"

"Maybe the shooter was in a hurry to get out of there," Wally said.

"How long does it take to pick up a casing?"

"You think it was left there on purpose?"

Hood shrugged. "Just brainstorming."

Wally remained silent for several beats, then asked, "You know what I think?"

Hood realized the question was rhetorical. He shook his head.

"I think we should sweep the area where Bishop's body was found. See if we can find another cartridge"

"Could be a wild goose chase." After the remains were discovered, Hood had contemplated intensifying the search, but dismissed the idea. He had reasoned the search party already had covered the area, the direction and distance of the gunshot were unknown, and time and weather would have affected—if not hidden or destroyed—any additional evidence.

"I know," Wally said, "but I won't be satisfied unless we give it a try."

"Okay," Hood said.

"Good. I'll reassemble the search team."

Hood rubbed the bagged cartridge between his fingers as he contemplated how to inquire among the Bishops, and Julian, about the rifle. "Can I keep this?"

"It's yours," Wally said.

As Hood bypassed the dispatcher's station on his way out the door, Maggie waylaid him.

He immediately guessed her intention, which she affirmed when she asked, "Have you had a chance to talk to

Linda or check your social media about the Citizens for Community Betterment people?"

Guilt washed over Hood as he searched in vain for a reasonable excuse. "Not yet," was the best he could do in the moment.

"But you will, right?"

"As soon as I get the chance," Hood said. "Promise."

"Okay," Maggie said. "Have a good evening."

"Thanks. You, too."

Although the early evening was calm as Hood crossed the parking lot, his thoughts felt scattered.

He pressed his key fob to unlock his vehicle, the brief beep followed by the sound of Young John's voice calling, "Hey boss, wait up."

Hood stopped, turned, and waited for his deputy to approach.

"Glad I caught you," Young John said.

"What's up?"

"I didn't want to bring this up in the office because I know you're a stickler for keeping department stuff and campaign stuff separate, but I heard something I thought you should know."

"Okay," Hood said.

"You know, I was at that training seminar in Sloan County yesterday and during one of the breaks, I got to talking with one of their deputies. He asked about the election campaign—said he'd heard about that Christmas party ad—and said something like, you know, that Grindell fellow's not so lily-white himself."

Hood squinted and wrinkled his nose to signal his confusion.

"As it turns out, this deputy's father and Grindell were college roommates, so the dad became interested after Grindell threw his hat in the sheriff's race. It wasn't until the race turned nasty that he made the comment about Grindell. The dad said during their junior year, Grindell got mixed up with some 'townie' and she got pregnant."

"Where are you going with this story, John?"

"The dad said Grindell dumped her when she told him she was having his baby. He called her a tramp and denied he was the father. He never helped in any way. He just finished his degree and left town."

"That's only one side of the story, John."

"Yeah, but you could check it out, see if it's—"

"And it was a long time ago."

"Well, the Christmas party photo they used against you was more than a year old."

Hood had no interest in arguing the point. "Thanks for the information," he said. He turned toward his cruiser.

"You gonna use it?" Young John asked.

Hood stopped and faced his deputy. "No."

"Why not?"

Hood considered his reasons. Even if the story could be verified, was it relevant? Did Grindell's decades-old behavior disqualify him as a candidate for sheriff? Would reviving the incident backfire? Would it be perceived by voters as an act of desperation by the sheriff? Hood's most compelling reason, however, was he had agreed to avoid negative campaigning.

All he said was, "Seems wrong."

"Do you know Susan Schulte?" Hood asked his wife as he stood at a counter in the kitchen.

"I know a Susan Schulte," Linda answered. "She's an administrator at the hospital—personnel or human relations or something—but Schulte is a pretty common name in Huhman County."

"That's the one."

The oven beeped, signaling it had reached the temperature Linda had selected.

"Why do you ask?" Linda opened the oven, placed a casserole dish on the center rack, and closed the door.

"Maggie's been doing some research on the Citizens for Community Betterment, the group that financed the Christmas Party ad. Susan Schulte was listed as a mutual friend of Maggie and one of three trustees."

"Who was the trustee?" Linda asked.

"Nancy Werdehausen, president of the group."

"Don't know her."

"I promised Maggie I'd do some research. Do I have time now or should I wait?"

"Go ahead," Linda said. "I'll call you."

Hood went to the den and sat at the home computer he and Linda shared; Elizabeth had her own laptop. He looked up the password—a combination of his wife's name and daughter's birthday—and logged onto the social media site.

In alphabetical order, he called up the names of the three officers. Constance "Connie" Bax, secretary, yielded no results. He was not "friends" with either Joe Miller, treasurer, or Nancy Werdehausen, president, but the limited biographies revealed Nancy Werdehausen's maiden name was Jacobs.

A synapse triggered in his brain. He knew he had heard or seen the name recently, but he couldn't recall where and when. Had he read it or had it come up in conversation? Was it connected to the case?

An answer seemed just on the periphery of his memory, but he couldn't bring it into focus. He repeated the name—Nancy Jacobs, Nancy Jacobs—in his mind.

Nothing.

"Dinner's ready," Linda called from the kitchen.

"Coming," Hood said. He shut down the computer and stopped to wash and dry his hands before returning to the kitchen. He was about to ask Linda if she knew Nancy Jacobs when he noticed his daughter's absence. "Where's Elizabeth?" he asked.

"She's at Claire's. It's just us tonight."

Hood glanced at the wall clock. "Isn't this early for dinner?"

"Well, you have your meeting tonight."

"Oh yeah." Hood filled a tumbler with ice water. "What're we having?"

"Chicken Parmesan."

As if on cue, a timer beeped and Linda took a bubbling entree from the oven and set it on the stovetop.

"Would you like a glass of wine?" Hood asked.

"No thanks. Water's fine."

Linda was not only what an alcoholic would characterize as a normal drinker, she was a lightweight; one glass of wine rendered her tipsy and giggly.

"You can have a glass of wine, you know," Hood said. "It won't bother me."

"I'm good. I don't need it."

"It's not a question of whether you need it. I'm asking if you want one."

Linda crossed the kitchen, reached out, and gripped her husband's forearm. "Why are you trying to pick a fight?"

"I'm not. I'm just saying you don't need to walk on eggshells around me."

"Am I doing something that makes you think that, because—if there is—I'm certainly not aware of it."

"I just feel like I'm being treated like some fragile, I don't know, something."

"You've been edgy lately, Francis." Linda released her grip. "Are you sure you're not projecting your own—"

"Like the meeting tonight, making dinner early so I don't have an excuse to skip it."

"I was just trying—"

"I didn't go last week," Hood blurted. "I left the house, but I didn't go to the meeting. I went to the Trestle, near the crime scene, and just sat on a log for an hour or so."

Linda said nothing.

"I didn't tell you, but I didn't lie, either. I never said I was going to the meeting."

"I thought you liked the meetings," Linda said.

"I do. It's just—"

A few beats of silence ensued before Linda asked, "It's just what?"

"I'm worried. That's all."

"About your recovery?"

"About everything. You know I love you," Hood said, "and Elizabeth. When you were away, it was like there was this void in my life. I didn't feel whole. And now—"

Linda waited. She knew not to rush him.

"I also love my job. I mean, it's got its ups and downs, but it's more than what I do. It's a part of me. And part of me feels like I'm going to lose it, that I'm going to lose the election, and I'm going to have to face that void again."

"You're not going to lose the election, Francis. You've proved yourself. You're well-liked, well-respected in this county. Admittedly, the Christmas Party ad was a setback, but—"

"I'm worried they're going to publicize that I'm an alcoholic."

"Who's they?"

"The Citizens for Community Betterment, or George Bishop, or Chip Luther—that bunch."

"Why would you think that?"

"Young John told me some stranger approached him and asked whether I go to meetings."

"Is that why you're having second thoughts about attending?"

"Exactly. I even talked to Matthew about it."

"What'd he say?"

"What he always says. He laid out the pros and cons and said it's my decision."

"Well, whatever it is," Linda said, "I support you."

Hood wrapped his arms around her and held her in a lengthy embrace. When he released her, he said, "Let's eat."

"Fear," Mac said. "You know, when I look back, I think I was afraid of getting sober."

Hood listened intently as Mac spoke during the weekly meeting.

As Mac continued, Hood watched an unfamiliar person descend the stairs and take a seat at the table. The sheriff wondered if the man—in his late twenties, perhaps early thirties—was new to recovery or, as sometimes happened, visiting from another group or from out of town.

"I wasn't sure recovery was in the cards for me," Mac said, "I'd pretty much resigned myself to the fact that I was destined to drink myself to death.

"But recovery still scared me. I was afraid of what my life would be like if I stopped and what would happen if I couldn't. I couldn't figure out why I kept relapsing until one of the old-timers pulled me aside and shared his experience about sabotaging his own recovery. That's when I realized I was victimizing myself. I was using self-sabotage to avoid facing my fear of sobriety. I was defeated, but I wasn't ready to surrender. I pass."

When it was Hood's turn to speak, he said, "When I first came in here, I was looking for how I was different from you, mainly because I wanted an excuse to walk away. The more time I spend here, however, the more I appreciate the similarities. Looking back, I also feared recovery. I led a double life as workaholic by day and alcoholic at night. My career carried lots of responsibilities, so I never drank on the job. But after work, I'd also drink until I passed out or blacked out.

"I started shirking my responsibilities at home and, gradually, my wife took them on. I don't think she meant to enable me. She just didn't want me driving our daughter or going to the store while I was impaired. Little by little, she took over the parenting duties and the household finances, in addition to the shopping, cooking, and cleaning. I was okay with that because, frankly, I just wanted to be left alone in the evenings.

"But," Hood continued, "living with an absentee husband and father, and watching him slowly destroy himself, got to be too much. She said if I didn't do something about my drinking, she'd take our daughter and leave. I didn't follow through. She did. But, as most of you know, that's not the end of the story. I stopped drinking nearly a year ago and my family and I recently reunited. That's all I've got."

The sharing continued clockwise around the table until it reached the newcomer, who was last to speak. "Hi, I'm

Tom," he said. "I'm just gonna pass tonight."

An alarm triggered in Hood's head. Was the stranger the same Tom who had approached Young John outside the courthouse? Was Tom infiltrating a recovery meeting to gather political dirt to use against Hood in the campaign?

As Matthew ended the session, again leading the group in reciting the Serenity Prayer, Hood bowed his head but continued watching Tom, who headed for the exit before the prayer ended.

Hood followed. He walked briskly but, by the time he reached the stairs, Tom had disappeared. Hood hurried up the stairs, climbing two at a time, rushed through the door and into the parking lot, where he saw taillights flash, signaling a vehicle was being unlocked by remote control.

"Hey," he called to Tom, who had opened the driver's side door. Hood expected the man to flee, but he didn't. He stood by the open car door and waited for Hood to approach.

"You said your name is Tom, right?" Hood asked.

"Yeah."

Hood extended his hand and Tom accepted the handshake.

"Do you know who I am?" Hood asked.

"I think you introduced yourself as Francis."

"That's right," Hood said. "Do you know what I do?"

"No. Why?"

"Not important. You from around here? I don't remember seeing you before."

"I'm from here in town, but this was my first meeting. I was pretty nervous. Did it show?"

"How'd you hear about us?"

"Friend of mine knows Matthew."

"Did you talk to a sheriff's deputy recently about meetings?"

"A deputy?"

"Outside the courthouse, where the sheriff's department is. He would have been in uniform."

"No."

Hood was confused. Tom was either a convincing liar or puzzled newcomer. The stranger's first name was Hood's only basis for suspicion. If he was an infiltrator, Hood considered, would he identify himself by the same name to both the deputy and the recovery group?

Hood decided to err on the side of caution. The last thing he wanted to do was falsely accuse—and perhaps drive away—a newcomer to recovery.

"It was nice to meet you, Tom," Hood said.

"You, too."

"And keep coming back," Hood said, adopting the slogan to encourage regular attendance at recovery meetings.

CHAPTER 22

Hood saw his own experience reflected in Kim's vacant stare.

After leaving the office, he had stopped by her hospital room. When he entered, she was curled in a fetal position beneath a tangle of blankets. Despite the covers, she was shaking uncontrollably and sweating profusely.

Hood was reminded of his early days of sobriety, when withdrawal from the physical cravings and mental obsession created a combustible mixture of sickness and misery. His only solace came from another slogan: *This too will pass.*

He wondered if Kim would find something similar to cling to during the storm of withdrawal. He wondered whether she was willing to surrender and ask for help.

"Sheriff," she said, a muttered whisper. She rolled slightly from her side to her back.

"I came by to see how you're doing."

"I feel like shit."

Hood adopted his most assuring tone. "It'll get better."

"Can't get worse."

Hood wasn't sure what to say. "Are they giving you anything, you know, for the—?" He left the question unfinished.

"Yeah, but I don't know what. Doesn't help much."

He lapsed into silence, unsure how lucid she was or

what she might remember.

"Nurses told me," she said, "you're the one who brought me in."

Hood nodded.

"They said it was a good thing. I'm guessing I might not have made it otherwise."

Hood shrugged.

Kim closed her eyes. Hood sensed the effort needed for the conversation had exhausted her.

Within minutes, her breathing indicated she was asleep.

He opened the door to leave, then turned and said, "I'll be around if you need me."

Hood was driving home when his cell phone sounded. The dashboard screen, synced to his phone, indicated the caller was Maggie. He activated the hands-free connection and said, "This is Francis."

"Did I call at a bad time?" she asked.

"This is fine."

"I've been doing more thinking about the Citizens for Community Betterment. We know the IRS allows the group to keep its donors secret, but its expenditures must be made public. For example, we know the group financed the Christmas Party ad, but not where it got the money."

"I'm with you," Hood said.

"But the group is limited to spending less than half of its donations on political activity, with the majority going to charitable causes, right?"

"Right."

"So, I asked myself—which charities?"

"I'm guessing groups that provide social services, youth services, senior services—"

"Exactly," Maggie said. "So, I got the list, and guess which group is the largest recipient?"

"No idea."

"The Mid-Missouri Foster Care and Adoption Association."

The disclosure hit Hood like a slap in the face. "Are you serious? That's the organization Anne Bishop works for."

"I'm as surprised as you are."

"I, um," Hood began, unable to form a response. "I need to give this some thought."

"I understand," Maggie said. "Just thought you'd want to know."

Hood was still puzzling through the ramifications of Maggie's disclosure when he entered his front door, beelined to the family room, and dropped into his recliner.

Linda folded the newspaper section she had been reading and laid it in her lap. "I heard some pretty good gossip today," she said.

Hood, who was trying to become a better listener, focused his attention on her. "You know my recovery program says I'm not supposed to engage in gossip."

"I thought that was gossiping about other members,"

Linda said. "What did you call it—taking another member's inventory?"

"Member or not, it's all the same."

"Does that mean you don't want to hear this? It's about your primary opponent." Linda's tone was a combination of chiding and teasing, but she had his attention.

"Let's hear it," he said.

"I was talking with a source on the county Republican committee today and she said Grindell has threatened to withdraw from the campaign if George Bishop and Chip Luther use some information they dug up."

"What information?" Hood asked, immediately assuming it was his alcoholism.

"I asked. My source didn't know. All she said was she heard Grindell told them he wanted no part of it. He told them if they publicized it, he'd withdraw."

Hood remained silent as he recalled Tom's presence at the recovery meeting.

"You think it's what you mentioned the other night?" Linda asked.

"I can't think of what else it could be," Hood said. "There was a new guy at the last meeting and I got really suspicious of his motives. Talk about taking someone else's inventory. I even followed him to the parking lot and chatted him up, but I really couldn't tell."

"But you think he could've been, like, a spy for the opposition?"

"I think Steve Grindell's a stand-up guy. Hell, his threat

to withdraw proves it. But I wouldn't put anything past those other guys."

"Even if he withdraws," Linda said, "it's too late to remove his name from the ballot."

"But if he says publicly that he's withdrawn—" Hood began.

"People could still vote for him. Plus, he'd be pressed to say why he withdrew. It could all get pretty messy."

"Does Otto know?" Hood asked.

"I haven't said anything to him."

Hood took his cell phone from his pocket. "I'd better call him."

"Remember," Linda said, "this is just what I heard from a single source."

Hood raised an index finger to signal his call had been answered. "Otto," he said. "It's Francis. Have you heard anything about Grindell withdrawing from the race?"

"No. What happened?"

Hood repeated what Linda had said.

"But she didn't hear why Grindell threatened to withdraw?" Otto asked.

"No, but I've got my own suspicions. I think George and Chip Luther are having me followed. I think they found out I go to recovery meetings and were planning to use it in the campaign. I think Grindell found out about it and used the only leverage he had."

"That's a lot of supposition, Francis. Do you have any proof?"

"No, but I feel it in my gut."

"I don't know that there's much we can do about it. Either they'll use it or they won't. Either it will make a difference or it won't. It could end up being counterproductive if voters don't like them dragging your personal life into this."

Hood considered what Anne had said about people's interest in what she had called his public/private paradox. "I need to step up the campaign," he told Otto. "What've we got—two weeks left?"

"Thirteen days," Otto said.

"Can we get together tomorrow night—your place, seven o'clock?" Hood asked. "In the meantime, I'll make a list of all the public events I can think of. We'll set up a schedule of where I need to be when."

"Sounds good. See you then."

Hood heard the unmistakable delight in his brother-in-law's tone as he disconnected.

CHAPTER 23

At Linda's suggestion, the campaign strategy session had been expanded into a family gathering, complete with homemade chocolate brownies, an apple pie, and iced tea and decaf coffee. Hood, Linda, and Elizabeth sat with Otto and Sarah at the oval table in the Kampeter kitchen.

"I don't have any polling data or demographics to base this on," Otto said, "but I'm guessing since Grindell was a police officer for so long, he'll have the greater name recognition in the city than the county."

"Makes sense," Hood said. He helped himself to a wedge of pie.

"There are five wards in the city, each with three precincts, for a total of fifteen," Otto continued. "Outside St. Gotthard, there are another fifteen county precincts. These include the unincorporated area and the small towns and villages."

"An even split," Elizabeth noted.

Hood glanced at his daughter, who seemed attentive. He smiled.

"So the question becomes," Otto added, "do we concentrate our efforts in the city or outside the city?" Before anyone could answer, he added, "Or do we try to do both?"

"With only two weeks left, do we have enough volunteers

and money to do both?" Linda asked.

"Good question," Otto answered. "I put a pencil to it this afternoon and came up with some options. We've got the money for a pretty strong series of newspaper ads, if Francis doesn't mind putting money in the Bishops' pockets. Television spots are more expensive, particularly during periods of high viewership—the news hour or prime time."

"I'm okay with newspaper ads," Hood said. "If people are paying for the paper, we can assume they're reading it. My cable TV bill isn't cheap, but even when the TV's on, there are sixty-some channels to watch. There's only one newspaper."

"I checked the newspaper's circulation numbers," Otto said. "It's been declining in recent years, as expected, but it's still pretty good in both the city and the county."

Elizabeth chimed in, "There's also a digital edition. We use it at school."

"I checked on that," Otto said. "The digital feature is free to print subscribers. Digital-only subscriptions are available, but the numbers aren't very impressive—at least, not yet. Maybe the next generation will—"

"I don't even want to think about a newspaper I can't fold," Linda said. "Would you have to print coupons in order to clip them or do you just show your phone at the checkout? And how would you do the crossword?"

"I'm with you, Linda," Otto replied. "We're living in a time of great change, which is not always easy for me. Look at this election. I suspect the Grindell camp has done polling, which was never done on a county level. And I can't imagine Chip Luther hasn't analyzed the demographics, although I can't imagine how productive that would be. I mean, in the last two elections, Francis ran unopposed once and won in a landslide over a Democrat."

"And," Sarah said, "we all know sighting a Democrat in the Huhman County Courthouse is rare."

"Exactly," Otto said. "And before Francis was appointed, I can't remember his predecessor ever facing opposition from either party. Cliff Westerman was an institution. But my point is I can't imagine there's much demographic data available on a Republican primary for sheriff."

"I'm sure Chip will come up with something to justify whatever the Bishops are paying him," Sarah sneered.

Otto gently refocused the discussion. "Let's get back to the campaign. What are some events coming up where we can be a presence, events that will draw a crowd?"

"Inside or outside the city?" Elizabeth asked.

"Both," Otto answered.

"The county commission is hosting a grand opening this weekend for its new paved trail around the lake at Huhman County Park," Linda said. "It's been well-publicized. I wouldn't be surprised if turnout is high."

"And," Hood said, "I know some of the candidates plan to set up campaign booths along the trail."

"Good." Otto made a note. "What else?"

"The local American Legion is hoping to finish its Veterans Plaza by the end of the month," Sarah added. "They had a dedication ceremony scheduled, but it was postponed because weather delayed construction."

"I'll put that down as a possibility," Otto said.

"Our cheerleading squad is hosting a car-wash fundraiser at the mall Saturday," Elizabeth said, "but it might be mostly high school kids who can drive but can't vote yet, so never mind."

"No. I'll add it to the list," Otto said. "Better to have too many options than not enough."

Hood was impressed with his brother-in-law's ability to validate every suggestion. No wonder Otto was so successful and well-liked in the community. Hood felt a renewed confidence in Otto's old-school—personal rather than digital—approach to the campaign.

The brainstorming session continued as pie slices and brownie squares disappeared, the iced-tea pitcher was drained, and a second pot of decaf was brewed and largely consumed.

"I think we've got a pretty good list," Otto said. "I'll verify dates and get back to you."

Sarah rose and began clearing the table, prompting everyone to join the cleanup. Linda stood at the sink rinsing dishes and handing them to Sarah, who loaded the dishwasher. As Hood carried plates to the counter, he told Otto what Maggie had learned about the Citizens for Community Betterment.

Otto listened attentively to Hood's summary, which he ended by identifying the group's trustees. "The president is Nancy Werdehausen, who used to be Nancy Jacobs. The name rings a bell, but—for the life of me—I can't place it."

"Did you say Nancy Jacobs?" Linda asked.

"Yes. Didn't I ask you already?"

"No." Linda rinsed a glass tumbler.

"Well, I meant to. I guess I forgot."

"There was a Nancy Jacobs in our high school graduating class," Linda said. "She was—"

"Nancy Jacobs," Hood nearly shouted, as the revelation flooded his memory.

"She was a chronic overachiever," Linda added. "Honor roll, field hockey captain, yearbook staff, prom decoration committee."

"Remember her campaign slogan when she ran for student council president our senior year? 'Just to set the record straight,' Hood began, with Linda joining in, 'Nancy Jacobs is great.'"

Otto, Sarah, and Elizabeth stared at the giddy twosome as if they had flipped their lids.

When they regained their composure, Linda said, "I don't know what their relationship is now, but Nancy Jacobs and Anne Bishop were best friends in high school."

"I remember," Hood said. "And I also remember where I heard the name. After we found the arm bone and I went to alert Marjorie, Anne met me and started reminiscing about high school. You know Anne's got the amazing memory condition. She started rattling off all kind of details about the graduation party at Nancy Jacobs' pool."

CHAPTER 24

The turnout for the grand opening of the paved trail at Huhman County Park surpassed Hood's expectations.

He remembered when the park was a densely wooded, largely inaccessible area surrounding a moderately sized, irregularly shaped lake. Only the most intrepid anglers would risk the hazards—ticks, poison ivy, snakes, and more—to reach the shore in hopes of landing a trophy largemouth.

Today, the grassy, mown expanse was dotted with oak, shagbark hickory, and cedar trees that shaded picnic tables and barbecue pits. The path circled the lake, which now hosted a ramp for fishermen and canoeists. A playground featured colorful equipment—including swings, slides, and a jungle gym—on a rubber-mulch surface designed to minimize injury.

Hood stood with the other county officials who had gathered for the dedication and watched as people shuffled their feet, awaiting the ceremonies.

He noted each of the county officials present faced opposition in the August primary or November general election. He also noted the candidates had set up campaign booths—spaced along the path—to distribute brochures, connect with voters, and pitch their platforms.

"I guess we'd better get started," said Huhman County

Presiding Commissioner Dan Sommerer. He stepped forward, adjusted the microphone, and said, "Thank you all for coming out today. We had no idea when we selected this date to unveil our newest amenity that the weather would cooperate, but we'll take it, right?"

Laughter and cheers abounded, encouraging the veteran politician and orator to continue his remarks. As soon as he sensed impatience among the crowd, however, he abbreviated his comments, but not before encouraging people to stop by the booths.

After the ceremonial ribbon was cut with the oversized scissors, Hood headed toward his booth, greeting people he knew and introducing himself to other potential voters.

His campaign stall was nothing more than a collapsible cloth canopy shading a plastic folding table and folding chair. As always, he was careful not to use any department-owned items or accessories for campaigning. He had purchased a plain, white portable canopy and table for multiple uses and he added signage in accordance with the event. To promote the D.A.R.E. program, for example, he affixed the anti-drug banner to the front of the table.

Today, he displayed his "Re-elect Sheriff Hood" sign and topped the table with a range of campaign materials—including free yardsticks, pocket combs, and brochures—all echoing the re-election message.

Some walkers obviously were exploring a new venue for their exercise routine; they focused on the trail and their pace was rapid. Others seemed to be meandering casually, enjoying the view, and stopping by the booths.

Between visitors, Hood chatted with the presiding commissioner who manned a neighboring booth. They agreed the turnout was "splendid," the weather was "exceptional," and the Cardinals were favored to make the playoffs if they didn't "blow their lead down the stretch."

Eventually, they settled into a silence that matched the lull in activity. Hood watched the walkers on the far side of the lake, rearranged his free paraphernalia, and contemplated his aversion to campaigning.

Other elected officials seemed to enjoy campaigning or at least claimed they did. Sommerer, for example, appeared to revel in the spotlight and enjoy glad-handing prospective voters.

Hood, however, couldn't find a way to share or muster such enthusiasm. He wondered why he had hauled and set up the canopy, table, chair, and campaign accessories to waste an entire afternoon groveling for, at best, a few votes?

The question had nattered at him since Linda revealed Grindell's offer to resign from the race on principle. Now, the answer came to him in a moment of epiphany. Grindell had proven himself a worthy challenger who deserved Hood's best effort.

Hood wondered why he hadn't grasped it before. Grindell was a stand-up guy, a capable law enforcement officer, a qualified candidate. If Hood wanted to keep his job—the job he loved—he needed to work for it. That's why he was here.

He sensed a presence across the table and looked up.

"Hello, Sheriff," Anne said.

"Hi," he said, his surprise apparent.

"Doing some campaigning, I see."

He nodded.

"How's it going?"

"Pretty slow. I was hoping more people would stop by."

Anne picked up a "Re-elect Sheriff Hood" pocket comb and ran her thumb along the plastic teeth. "I mean, how's it going overall?"

Hood wasn't sure how to answer. "What's your impression?" he asked.

She shrugged and replaced the comb on the table. "Hard to say, but you can count on my vote."

"Thanks." Hood looked past her to see if anyone else was waiting to approach, but no one was. "So, what brings you out here?" he asked, trying to make his curiosity sound conversational.

"I wanted to have a look at the new trail. Foster and adoptive parents are always looking for places to spend time, interact, and get to know their new children."

Hood nodded.

"Anything new with the investigation?" Anne asked.

Hood had anticipated the question, but his customary reluctance to share information kicked in. "Nothing substantial," he answered.

"But you'll let us know?"

He appreciated her use of the word "us." His responsibility was not just to Anne, but to the entire family. Sharing information, however, was a tightrope when family members remained potential suspects. His intention was to share as many details with as many family members as possible, without compromising the case. "Of course," he replied.

"Well, I'll be on my way," she said.

As she turned to leave, Hood said, "Wait."

She turned and faced him.

He wanted to ask if she was familiar with military ammo and sniper rifles, if she remained close to Nancy Jacobs—now Werdehausen—and if she was aware of the donations to her agency from the Citizens for Community Betterment. He realized, however, this was neither the time nor place.

"Never mind," he said.

Kim was sitting in the bedside chair when Hood framed himself in the open door of her hospital room. Beside her was a tray table with empty plates and torn wrappers, obviously left over from lunch.

"Can I come in?" he asked.

She nodded to a second seat facing the foot of the bed and perpendicular to her.

He entered, sat, and removed his hat. "How are you?"

"They say the worst is over. They're giving me some drugs—how weird is that?—and they want me to start some program, New Directions or something."

"New Opportunities," Hood said.

She lifted a brochure from the tray table. "Yeah, that's

right. I read the brochure they left during lunch." She creased her brows as if retrieving a memory. "Is that the thing you told me about that time you came out to see me?"

"Yes."

"You knew I was fucked up?"

Hood scrunched his mouth to eliminate his perpetual smile and nodded.

"But that's not why you came the second time?"

"I had some questions."

"About what?"

"About the Sunday morning James Bishop disappeared. I know you were back in town. I have a witness who saw Julian's truck about 2 a.m. that Sunday, and when I told Julian, he confirmed it."

"Well, I guess that cat's out of the bag."

"He said the reason he drove back is because you needed a fix."

"That's true," Kim said. She looked at her plate, avoiding Hood's gaze. "Julian won't let me take drugs on the road because he's afraid we'll get stopped. So, I got high before we left and figured that would hold me long enough. It didn't. I started coming down and I knew there was no way I'd be able to sleep in the truck, so I begged him to drive home. He was pissed but he did it."

"What time did you get back?"

"I don't know. Two sounds about right."

"Then what?"

"I took care of it, got myself right. I mean, it wasn't even about getting high at that point. It was just getting normal."

Hood breathed deeply, saddened by the notion that equated impairment with normalcy. "Julian said he gave you his keys so you could meet your dealer."

"He gave me his keys before he crashed. I guess he assumed I needed to score, but I didn't. I had my own stash at home."

"You didn't take his truck and go out on your own that morning?"

"No. Why would I? Like I said, I had my own stash."

Hood looked into Kim's eyes, at the clarity that had replaced the previous cloudiness. The question—*Who do you trust?*—resonated in his thoughts. He wanted to trust her but feared that was only because he wanted to see the addict as a victim, not a suspect. He picked up the New Opportunities brochure on her tray table. "You going to give this a try?"

She shrugged. "What have I got to lose?"

"This was nice," Linda said.

She sat across from her husband in a booth at Derek's, still nursing the glass of Cabernet she had ordered when they were seated. Hood sipped his second tumbler of ice water, garnished with a slice of lemon, as they waited for their plates to be cleared. A small hurricane candle between them began to flicker.

"It was Elizabeth's idea," Hood confessed. Although Linda lifted her glass to mask her expression, Hood realized she knew their daughter had instigated the dinner date. "It was nice," he added, attempting to mask the lie. He had felt uneasy throughout the evening. And the more he tried to pinpoint the cause, the more frazzled he became. On top of everything, he began to scold himself for his selfish behavior on his wife's birthday, magnifying his discomfort.

"How's everything at work?" Linda asked.

Hood maintained a compartmentalized approach to his work. Although he discussed election strategy with Linda, or shared occasional anecdotes about Maggie's grandchildren or Wally's spirited sons, shop talk was reserved for his staff. He shrugged. "Is that what you really want to talk about?"

"I want to talk about whatever is bothering you."

"Is it that obvious?"

"We've known each other a long time, Francis. I can read signals."

"I never could hide things from you," he conceded. "You always knew when I'd been drinking."

"I could see it in your eyes." She sipped her wine. "Now what's going on?"

"Anne Bishop kissed me." Although he surprised himself by blurting the words without preamble, he was not nearly as stunned as Linda was to hear them. After several beats of awkward silence, he added, "It was just a kiss on the cheek. Maybe she meant it as a harmless greeting after all these years."

"When did it happen?"

"A couple days ago when I went to the estate. I didn't tell you then, but it's been bothering me ever since."

Linda lifted her glass but didn't drink. "Are you bothered by what happened or because you didn't tell me right away?"

"Both, I guess. I'd be lying if I said I wasn't flattered. Anne Bishop was the 'it' girl in high school. She never paid any attention to me, and now—out of nowhere—she kissed me on cheek. It was an ego boost—that's for sure—but I feel guilty for some reason."

Linda leaned forward. "You're a good man, Francis. I trust you. Even when you were at your worst—when the drinking dominated your life—I knew you could never cheat. You have principles, and even the thought of violating them tears you up. You couldn't even keep a peck on the cheek a secret for very long."

Hood was about to respond when their waitress approached the booth and began removing their dinner plates. "Any room for dessert tonight, folks?"

"I'm good," Linda said.

Hood looked at his wife. "We're good."

CHAPTER 25

As Hood crossed the hospital parking lot, he pressed the button on his plastic key fob to unlock his vehicle. The lights flashed in synchronicity with the ring tone of his cell phone. The screen indicated the caller was Wally.

"Hood," he answered, skipping his usual "this-is-your-sheriff" response.

"We found it," Wally said, his tone bright with elation.

Hood immediately knew what Wally meant by "it"—another 5.56-mm NATO bullet casing.

"Great. Where'd you find it?"

"On a knoll about a hundred yards from where Bishop's remains were found. It would have been a perfect vantage point."

Hood thought of what Loeffelman had said about the trajectory—the bullet traveled at a slightly downward angle from front to back. "Want me to head out there?"

"No need," Wally said. "I've already bagged it. I'm on my way to the crime lab now."

"I'll leave you to it, then."

"Okay. See you in the morning."

"See you then." Before disconnecting, Hood added, "Great job, by the way."

* * * * *

The format for the second debate was largely unchanged from the first.

The moderator again sat in the judge's chair, but the candidates' seats were switched; Grindell occupied the witness box and Hood sat in the stenographer's seat. The trio of reporters again included the *Tribune's* Wadkins, but the reporters from local radio and television stations were different.

After the moderator's introductions, each candidate opened with a prepared statement. Grindell was first. Hood listened attentively as his opponent largely repeated his previous opening statement.

When it was Hood's turn, he began with revised remarks, focusing on his background and experience, his commitment to county residents, and his passion for serving and protecting them. Gone was any trace of nervousness or anxiety. He spoke from his heart.

The questioning began with KMIS-TV reporter Doug Stieferman asking the candidates about their responses to a recent rash of vandalism, including damaging vehicles, defacing buildings, and toppling tombstones in a parish cemetery.

Grindell was first to answer and, as Hood expected, he stressed law and order and emphasized stronger punishment as a deterrent.

When it was Hood's turn, he looked directly into the camera and spoke. "Make no mistake. I take these incidents of vandalism very seriously. I, myself, and the sheriff's department, are making every effort to identify and arrest the perpetrators. And we will.

"But, as I've said regarding other crimes largely involving young people, instruction is paramount. Vandalism is recorded as a crime against property, not a crime against a person, like assault or robbery. But vandalism is not a victimless crime. When a vehicle or building is vandalized, someone's sense of security is damaged as well. When a church or cemetery is vandalized, someone's belief in basic human decency is threatened.

"Vandalism," Hood continued, becoming more animated, "has no reward. It is, if anything, some misguided sense of fun, usually fueled by alcohol or drugs. The damage is just that—damage. Nothing is gained, but something is lost. From any standpoint, it's inane behavior. It flies in the face of social mores, criminal laws, and the Golden Rule. And for what?

"That's why we must instruct young people—in our homes, our schools, our churches, our institutions—that vandalism is doing to others what you would not like them to do to you. It's pointless."

Hood finished and the questioning continued, largely focused on the candidates' public safety policies or approaches to specific crimes. Nothing challenging or unexpected occurred during the final round of questions until the rotation came to Wadkins.

"Capt. Grindell," the *Tribune* reporter began, "I looked over the most recent campaign finance reports each of you is required to make public and I saw that the lion's share of your donations came from two sources—James Bishop Jr., who goes by Jay, and his younger brother, George. Are you aware of that?"

"Yes," Grindell said. His perfunctory answer suggested he had no intention of elaborating.

"For the record," the reporter continued, "I'd like to point out that both men are board members and officers of the *St. Gotthard Tribune*, my employer. I'd also like to point out that they did not request and, to my knowledge, are unaware I would ask you about these contributions. My question is, if elected, would you feel any allegiance or pressure to adhere to any editorial policies advocated by the newspaper regarding law enforcement?"

Hood—who was surprised and impressed that Wadkins asked the question—looked to Grindell to gauge his reaction.

"Absolutely not," Grindell said, his voice and manner calm. "The Bishops have been good corporate citizens. Jay and George provide jobs and paychecks to a number of county residents, including—as you pointed out—yourself. Furthermore, I am familiar with their editorial policies and I share the common sense, no-nonsense approach to fighting crime promoted by their father, and now, by them."

Hood surmised from Grindell's demeanor he had anticipated and rehearsed his answer.

"I knew the boys' father," Grindell continued, "and I've gotten to know the children, particularly Jay and George. That said, they know if we do differ on policy matters, I am my own man and I will make my decisions based on what I believe is in the best interest of the people of Huhman County."

"What do you know about what has become known as the Christmas Party ad, financed by the Citizens for Community Betterment?" Wadkins asked. "I was able to contact the group's treasurer, Joe Miller, who claims it's a tax-exempt 501-(c)(4) organization established to address social issues and influence public policy."

"I don't know anything about that. Quite frankly, I never heard of that group until I saw the ad in the paper."

Wadkins' expression revealed his dissatisfaction with the answer. "Thank you, Captain." He turned to Hood and said, "Sheriff, how do you respond to donors who expect or pressure you to conform to their beliefs regarding criminal justice?"

"As I always have," Hood said. "I remind them that a majority of voters elected me because they had confidence in the principles and strategies I laid out during my campaign. Having served in the department for more than twenty years, the last nine as sheriff, I also have a record of performance people can judge. But generally, I agree with what my opponent said about this office or, for that matter, any public office. We have a responsibility to honestly tell voters what we hope to do and, if elected, to do it. If we're criticized and realize we're wrong, we change and grow. But that's not the same as swaying in the breeze of public opinion."

"Well said. Thank you, Sheriff," Wadkins said.

Hood basked in the compliment. The *swaying in the breeze* phrase had come to him spontaneously.

"I'm afraid that's all the time we have for questions," the moderator announced. "Each candidate will now have two minutes for final statements. We'll begin with Sheriff Hood."

The statements were anticlimactic rehashes of previous points. Hood waited until the television lights went out and people began to mingle before leaving the stenographer's seat. He was pleased with his debate performance. His smile broadened and a buoyancy lightened his step as he crossed the chamber and offered his hand to Grindell.

Anne peered through the rectangular leaded-glass window in her front door, then pulled it open in answer to the knock. "Francis," she said. "I wasn't expecting you."

"Good morning," Hood said. "Thought I'd stop and give you an update."

"How'd you know I was home?"

"I didn't, but I was in the area, so—" He shrugged, leaving the sentence incomplete.

"Well, come in." Anne opened the screen door. "Want some coffee?"

"I don't want to put you to any trouble."

"Nonsense. I'll join you for a cup. I think the warmer shut off, but I can zap some."

"Okay." Hood followed her into the kitchen and sat at the table in the same chair he had occupied during his previous visit.

"So, what's new?" She took a cup from the cabinet, filled

it with coffee, and reheated it in a microwave.

"Did you know Kim, Julian's former girlfriend, is in the hospital?" he asked.

"Actually, I did." The microwave buzzed. Anne removed the cup of steaming coffee and placed it on the table in front of Hood. "Julian told me. He heard she overdosed. He also said you were the one who found her."

Hood nodded.

"Good thing you went out there." Anne put a second cup in the microwave and repeated the process. "Were you planning to arrest her?"

"For what?"

"Julian said he told you they didn't stay overnight in Iowa. He said he admitted the alibi was phony and Kim borrowed his truck early Sunday morning. He figures she was trying to squeeze money out of my stepfather and had something to do with his death."

Hood sipped coffee, looking over his cup at her before he said, "That's one explanation."

"But you don't think so?"

"What's your theory for how she would go about squeezing money out of him? Some kind of fraud or blackmail maybe?"

"I don't know. Maybe she made up something," Anne said. Then, as if the concept had taken shape in her mind, she added, "Maybe she threatened to claim my stepfather was having an affair with her."

"Interesting," Hood said. "Do you think that would work?"

"I don't know."

"But you knew your stepfather pretty well. How do you think he'd respond to such a threat?"

"I think he'd try to fix the problem. That's what he did. James was a fixer." Anne sipped her coffee. "Maybe that's what happened. James arranged to meet with Kim to discuss it, maybe they met out by the Trestle, and they got into an argument, a fight, and she shot him."

"Possible, but not provable." Hood sipped coffee, holding his cup near his mouth.

"What's your theory?" Anne asked.

"I'm not at the theory phase yet. I'm still scratching around for evidence." He placed his cup on the table. "Speaking of evidence, do you have a gun collection?"

She hesitated before answering, "Yes."

"May I see it?"

"Whatever for?"

"I'm interested."

Anne shrugged and removed keys from her purse. "Follow me."

Hood trailed her through the living room and into a room that apparently doubled as spare bedroom and study. Against a wall was a glass-fronted gun cabinet fully stocked with 12 rifles.

"What exactly are you looking for?" she asked, as she unlocked and opened the double doors.

"A weapon that fires a 5.56 NATO cartridge, possibly a military rifle."

"Sorry," she said. "Can't help you. My marksman rifles use .338s. I've shot my stepbrother's rifle. It fires 5.56 ammo. Not a fan."

"Which stepbrother?"

"Jay. He had it out at the range one day. He told me to give it a try and asked what I thought."

"Do remember what kind of rifle it was?"

"Of course," Anne said. Hood watched her expression change as she seemed to retrieve data from some distant memory vault. "It's a Squad Advanced Marksman Rifle, also called SAM-R," she continued. "It was developed by the Marine Corps for use during Operations Desert Storm and Enduring Freedom, but it's since been taken out of service." She sipped coffee. "What does this have to do with evidence?"

"I'm sorry," Hood said, still mesmerized by her recall.

"You said 'speaking of evidence,' then asked about rifles."

"I'm not at liberty to say." Hood's intent was to gauge her reaction, not disclose information.

Anne gestured to the open gun safe. "Are you done?" she asked.

Hood nodded and she secured the doors. As she led him back to the kitchen, she said, "Well, I'm sure Jay isn't the only person who owns that kind of rifle. People sell them at gun shows all the time."

When they returned to their seats, Hood asked, "You ever get one of those song lyrics—or a slogan or something—stuck in your head and it just keeps repeating over and over?"

"Sure," Anne answered. "I think it's called an earworm.

For me, though, I never have trouble remembering the name of the song, the lyrics, the artist, even where I was and what I was doing the first time I heard it. It can be maddening."

"You know what's been running through my head lately?"

"No idea."

"Just to set the record straight, Nancy Jacobs is great."

Hood watched as Anne repeated her memory-retrieval process. "That's not a song, that was her student council campaign slogan our senior year."

"I know," Hood said, "but I'd forgotten about it until you reminded me of the pool party she hosted on graduation night."

"It's kind of corny, but it is catchy."

"As I recall, you and Nancy were best friends in high school."

"We were. You have a good memory."

Hood appreciated the irony of the compliment. "Do you still keep in touch?"

"Not enough. We're in a book club together, but sometimes she skips, or I do. We're both pretty busy. I haven't seen her since—" she hesitated momentarily, "the May 12 meeting at Joan Dulle's house."

"Did you know Nancy is president and one of three trustees of Citizens for Community Betterment?"

Anne stiffened noticeably. "What about it?"

"I was wondering if you, as executive director of the Mid-Missouri Foster Care and Adoption Association, were aware Nancy's group is among the largest benefactors of your organization?"

"I wouldn't exactly call it my organization any more than I would call Citizens for Community Betterment Nancy's group. Besides, I thought you came to update me about the case, not discuss your campaign."

Hood noted Anne's answers had become more cryptic, her tone more defensive. "Fair enough," he said, hoping to avoid confrontation.

"Look," Anne said. "I know the Citizens group financed the Christmas Party ad, but I want you to know I had nothing to do with that. I don't know if my brothers were involved in that, if they gave money. I don't—" She raised her hands, palms up, in a gesture of surrender. "I don't know anything."

"Neither do I," Hood said. "The organization is set up like a dark money group that isn't required to identify its contributors."

Anne stood. "I need to get ready for an appointment." She peered into his coffee cup. "Are you finished?"

Hood knew the conversation was over. "Thanks for the coffee," he said, as he handed her the empty cup. "I'll be in touch."

CHAPTER 26

"I've got news," Wally said. He stood in the open doorway to his boss's office.

"Me too," Hood replied.

Wally entered and sat. "You first."

"Okay. Anne told me her brother, Jay, owns a military rifle that fires a 5.56 NATO cartridge. She said she tried it out at the gun range. Your turn."

"I just heard from Sandra at the crime lab. The two casings—the one from the crime scene and one from the range—were fired by the same gun. She said something about matching firing pin marks and breech face striations, but she lost me."

Hood leaned backward in his chair, pondering the information.

"And," Wally added, "she found Jay's fingerprints—right thumb and index finger—on the casing from the crime scene."

"Let me make sure I've got this straight," Hood said. "Jay's prints are on the crime scene casing but there were no prints on the firing range casing. Why the difference?"

"We figured the shooter at the gun range wore gloves."

"Which made sense at the time. But now the question

arises—why didn't the person who killed James wear gloves?"

"Different shooters?" Wally speculated.

"Maybe," Hood said. "All I know is something doesn't add up. Jay's an intelligent man. I can't picture him using his own rifle to kill his father, then leaving behind a bullet casing with his prints on it. It's like leaving a calling card that says 'arrest me.'"

"So what's our next step?"

"It's time to have the crime lab analyze Jay's rifle."

Hood and Wally stood on the threshold of what a real estate agent might describe as an executive home. He didn't know much about architecture, but he suspected the recurring exterior arches—featured in the brick portico, large windows, and oak doorway—enhanced a specific style, as well as the price of the home.

Hood pressed the doorbell.

Jay opened the door and registered surprise at both the presence of the lawmen and the oblong cardboard box held by Wally. "Sheriff, Deputy?"

"May we come in?" Hood asked.

"I guess," Jay answered. He stepped aside, allowing Hood and Wally to enter. "What's going on?"

"I understand you own a SAM-R rifle that fires 5.56 NATO ammunition. I'm here to collect it. I have a warrant."

"Fine with me," Jay said. "Let me show you where I store it."

Hood and Wally trailed Jay into an airy room that

elaborated on the overall theme, with arched windows and doorways. Diane sat on one end of a plush, red sofa and leafed through a magazine. She greeted the sheriff, but eyed Wally quizzically.

After Hood made introductions, Diane asked, "What's in the box?"

"It's empty," Hood said.

As if to prove the point, Wally set the box on the carpet and opened it. As he withdrew to an inconspicuous position near the doorway, Hood moved to the center of the room and addressed the couple. "Do you keep your house locked when you're away?"

"Of course," Jay answered.

"Any break-ins at your home in the past year?"

Jay looked to Diane. Both seemed baffled by the question. "No," Jay answered.

"Does anyone else have access to your home? Any family members, for example, have a key or a pass code to the garage?"

Jay contemplated the question. "My family does."

"Who, specifically?"

"Mom, Anne, George. I think Henry gave me his key before he moved."

"Julian?" Hood asked.

"No."

Hood gestured to an ornate walnut gun cabinet in a corner of the room. "Is that where you keep the rifle?"

Yes?"

"Has it been broken into or have any items been stolen

from it in the past year?"

"No."

"Is it kept locked?"

"Always."

"Show me where you keep the key, but please don't touch it."

Jay walked to a grandfather clock on the opposite side of the room, opened the front panel, and pointed to a key hanging from a small nail. Hood noted the key was not visible until the panel was opened. He pulled on gloves and removed the key, then crossed to the gun cabinet and unlocked it.

"That's the SAM-R on the far right," Jay said.

Hood removed the rifle, laid it in the cardboard box, and put on the lid.

"If you're looking for fingerprints," Jay said, his tone betraying anxiety, "you're going to find mine all over that gun."

"I expect to," Hood said. He stood, relocked the cabinet, put the key in a plastic bag, and pocketed it. "We have your prints on file from our initial investigation last year."

"Are you going to tell me what this is all about?"

Hood looked from Jay to Diane. Both wore expressions revealing fear and confusion. "I'm sorry," he said. "I wish I could, but this is an ongoing investigation." His words sounded hollow, even to him.

CHAPTER 27

When he arrived at the Bishop estate, Hood introduced himself to the woman who had identified herself on the intercom as Connie. After some miscommunication, she had consulted with Marjorie and opened the main gates.

Hood guessed Connie was Latina, but he was clueless about her country of origin. She escorted him to a fieldstone patio, where Marjorie sat in a white, wrought-iron chair at an oval table with a glass top. An umbrella through the center of the table offered shade for both Marjorie and Danielle, who snuggled in her lap. The pom looked up when Hood and Connie approached, then signaled disinterest by nestling anew.

"What a pleasant surprise," Marjorie said to the sheriff. "Would you join me for some iced tea?" She gestured to the pitcher and tall glass, both condensing and creating rings of water on the tabletop.

"I will, thank you."

She nodded to Connie, then invited the sheriff to sit.

As Connie departed, Hood sat across the table from Marjorie, but neither of them spoke immediately.

Marjorie seemed content to survey the expansive yard. Hood settled into the silence. He was in no hurry to ask questions. He still wasn't entirely sure why he had come or what he hoped to learn. He decided his first order of business was to determine whether Marjorie was having one of her good days, a euphemism for her mental acuity.

Their quiet reverie was interrupted when Connie returned with a glass that matched Marjorie's and filled it from the pitcher.

"Thank you, Connie," Marjorie said, tacitly permitting her to resume whatever chore she had interrupted.

"How long has Connie been here?" Hood asked.

"The children hired her after my husband disappeared—I mean, after it was long enough for us to accept he might not be coming back. They claimed I needed help around the house, but I think the real reason was they didn't want me to get lonely."

"Your family, um, your children," Hood began, searching for the right words. "They seem to look out for you."

"They're wonderful. I don't know what I'd do without them."

"Did they get along with your husband, you know, the same way?"

Marjorie's expression clouded. Hood wasn't sure if she was contemplating the question or trying to understand its meaning.

Just as he was about to clarify, she said, "It's different between mothers and fathers, and between sons and daughters, too."

"How so?"

"James was the provider who managed the family business

and dealt with things out there. I was the nurturer, the protector who tended to things at home. I think they respected James, but when they needed comfort, they came to me."

"It looks like Jay is making a smooth transition into your husband's role at the newspaper. You must be very proud of him."

"Of course, but I wish Anne and Henry hadn't left. They could have been very helpful to him. They have traits he lacks. I think he'll realize that in time."

Hood had assumed each left to pursue an individual passion, not to distance themselves from Jay or his management style. "Why do you think they left?" he asked.

"For Henry, it just wasn't his thing. For Anne, it was different."

"Different how?"

"I think she got tired of being bossed by the men."

Hood remained silent, hoping she would elaborate.

"As you know, James isn't Anne's father," Marjorie said. "What you may not know is her father abandoned us after I told him I was pregnant. We've never contacted each other, and Anne has never asked about him. She was bitter, and scarred, for a long time. I don't know if she's found a way to deal with that or if she's been able to put it behind her, but I do know she bristles at taking orders from men."

Marjorie lifted the pitcher and refilled her glass. "More tea, Sheriff?

Hood declined, wordlessly waving his hand above his glass.

"My husband could be very demanding," Marjorie continued. "He had a way of getting what he wanted, and what he wanted was for the children to carry on the family business. He also wanted it to be under Jay's leadership. I think that left a bad taste in Anne's mouth."

"Because she's the oldest," Hood said.

"She's not only the oldest, she's the smartest. But she isn't a Bishop by birth and she isn't male."

The reasoning struck Hood as a medieval notion that somehow had survived, even thrived, in modern times.

"But my husband also was frustrated." Marjorie said. "I sensed it. He couldn't decide if leaving the business to the children would be a blessing or a curse. He knew the industry needed to change to survive, but success stories were few and far between. Jay had proposed the new printing plant as a survival tool, but James was struggling with that—"

"Hello," Anne said, interrupting and startling her mother.

"Anne," Marjorie said. "I wasn't expecting you."

Anne stood in the doorway separating the interior from the patio. "I just thought I'd stop by," she said. She turned to Hood. "Hello, Sheriff."

"Anne," he said, acknowledging her presence.

An awkward silence prevailed until Marjorie said, "The sheriff and I were just enjoying some iced tea and conversation. Do you have time to join us, dear?"

"I think I will," Anne said. "I'll get a glass." She disappeared indoors.

Hood suspected Anne's visit wasn't coincidental. Before

she returned, he asked Marjorie, "Does Anne often drop by in the afternoon during the work week?"

"She's here a lot on the weekends, but rarely during the week. And, usually, she calls first."

"I was told," Hood said, "you have good days and bad, but I guess I must be lucky, because you seem to be having a good day every time I've seen you recently."

"Who said that?" Marjorie asked.

Anne's reappearance on the patio precluded Hood from answering. Anne filled her glass from the pitcher and sat perpendicular to her mother and the sheriff. "So," she asked, "what have you two been talking about?"

"Actually," Hood said, preempting Marjorie from answering, "we've been enjoying a nice conversation." He raised a finger to signal he had more to say, lifted his glass with his other hand, and sipped tea. "We've been talking about the family, the newspaper, the future of the industry." He set his glass on the table. "I guess you could say we were talking about everything."

Anne turned to Marjorie. "How are you feeling today, Mother?"

"I'm fine, dear. Thank you for asking."

Anne redirected her attention to Hood. "Did you arrive at any solutions to save the newspaper industry? Something none of us has been able to come up with?"

Hood detected a hint of derision in her tone. "Hardly," he said. "I guess the best idea I've heard is Jay's proposal to build a printing plant."

"I call it 'Jay's folly,'" Anne said. "We'll never make enough to pay off the debt."

"What do you think, Marjorie?" Hood asked.

"I don't care, as long as the children can agree."

"I take it they're not of one mind," Hood said.

"Jay and George support the new plant," Anne answered. "Henry and I have reservations, just like mother."

Hood folded his hands. "Where did James stand on all this?" The sheriff watched as Anne and Marjorie stared at each other. Neither appeared eager to tackle the question.

"I honestly don't know," Marjorie said, finally. "Obviously, he was considering the possibility. I mean, he was looking at possible sites, but I know he was torn."

"I think," Anne added, "he wanted to side with Jay, but it was against his better judgment." She sipped tea, then added, "And I think Jay resented it."

CHAPTER 28

Hood entered the activities room at Our Lady of Help Catholic Church and displayed his voter registration card to the election authorities.

No lines had formed. Turnout for the primary, as predicted, was light.

The sheriff exchanged pleasantries with the poll workers as one examined his card and asked him to sign his name on the roster of registered voters.

"Democrat or Republican ballot, Sheriff?" a second poll worker quipped.

"Tough decision," Hood said, playing along. "Think I'll stick with the Grand Old Party."

He felt his cell phone vibrate in his pocket. He removed it and looked at the display, which indicated the call was from Sandra at the crime lab. He decided to return her call as soon as he exited the polling place.

He carried the ballot to a long table, where privacy was provided by a series of cardboard dividers resting on the surface. He sat in a metal folding chair and picked up the supplied black ink pen, then paused.

Thoughts about competition versus cooperation squared off in his mind. He and Grindell were competing to be elected sheriff. Hood had come to think of the position as his job, but it wasn't his. He didn't possess it. He earned it only by winning a popular vote every four years.

He realized, however, that he had come to think of it as his—in the sense that he had allowed the job to define who he was. He was sheriff. He introduced himself as sheriff; he greeted people on the phone by saying, "This is your sheriff."

Although he had thought his use of the phrase showed humility, he now realized the opposite was true. In his mind, he was introducing himself not as a public servant, but as a titled leader.

He also realized he had allowed his persona as sheriff to overshadow other aspects of his life. He also was a husband, father, relative, co-worker, and friend, but he thought of himself primarily as sheriff—a role accompanied by authority, respect, and control.

And it was that part of himself he was on the threshold of losing. When he started recovery, he had feared losing control through the act of surrender. Now, he faced losing the election and the authority inherent in the position.

He understood his reluctance to campaign was an excuse. He was afraid to lose, but he was also afraid of losing face.

A part of him felt he no longer deserved to be sheriff. He had descended into alcoholism during his tenure. He had allowed his life to get out of balance. He had let his drinking diminish every aspect of it—relationships with family and friends, his attitudes and behaviors, his duties and responsibilities. Instead of facing life, he had used alcohol to escape.

What, he wondered, was he escaping from—his dreams, aspirations, failures, fears, guilt?

He stared at the blank ballot.

He told himself he should feel good about choosing recovery, but he knew he had only started to repair the damage done. He remembered someone in his recovery group referring to himself as a physical, mental, emotional, and spiritual being.

In his mind, body, heart, and soul, Hood believed he was making progress. But, at this moment, he believed Grindell might be the better candidate. He hoped, in time, his thinking would change.

"Hello, Francis," Sandra said. "Thanks for returning my call."

"Of course."

"The rifle you asked to me examine fired both your NATO casings."

"I'm not surprised."

"And the gun was clean—I mean clean—inside and out. There were no prints, not even partials."

"You mean in addition to Jay's, right."

"I mean none, zero. All I found were fibers, probably from a cleaning cloth."

Silence reigned while Hood pondered the information.

"Francis, you still there?"

"Yes," he answered. "I'm just trying to figure out what that means."

"It looks to me as if someone intentionally wiped it clean."

"Okay," Hood said. He was still baffled. "Thanks."

Hood drove directly to the *St. Gotthard Tribune*, announced himself at the front desk, and was directed to Veronica Snellen, Jay's administrative assistant.

"I'm here to see Jay. I mean Mr. Bishop. I don't have an appointment, but it will only take a few minutes."

"One moment." She called her boss, repeated Hood's request, then said, "He's free. Go on in."

Hood entered, exchanged a handshake across the desk, then asked, "Do you remember when you last cleaned the SAM-R rifle?"

"I believe it was the Monday before last. It was one of two guns I had taken to the range that weekend."

"You're certain?"

"Yes. I try to go to the range each weekend when I'm not traveling, and I always take time on Monday to clean the guns I use."

Hood calculated Jay's cleaning preceded the errant shot at the gun range. "Did you use a cloth to wipe the rifle?"

"Yes."

"Did you wear gloves?'

"No. Why?"

"So, as far as you know, your fingerprints from when you handled the gun and put it back in the cabinet would still be on the gun."

"Sure. That's why I told you at the house that you'd find my prints all over it." Jay eyed the sheriff quizzically. "What's going on?"

"I'm not sure," Hood said, although he knew what had happened—someone else had wiped the gun clean. What he didn't know was who or why.

Linda stepped out of the van her husband had parked in the lot at the Lion's Den, the site Otto had chosen for the election watch party. She opened her umbrella to shelter herself from the drizzle and lingered before closing the door. When Hood failed to unfasten his seat belt, she peered inside and asked, "Are you coming?"

"I need a minute," he replied.

She perched on the passenger seat, holding the open umbrella above the open door of the van. "No rush," she said. "I understand."

When the silence between them—punctuated by the persistent drizzle—became uncomfortable, Hood said, "You know, Steve Grindell could make a pretty good sheriff."

"Not as good as you."

"I appreciate that."

"You've done all you can," Linda said. "What's the phrase? 'It's all over but the shouting.'"

"Or is it: 'It's all over but the crying?'"

"Well, we'll know soon enough."

"You know what's weird?"

"What?" she asked.

"You'd think the election outcome would be the main

thing on my mind, but it's not."

Linda remained silent, puzzled by the comment.

"What I can't stop turning over in my mind is why Anne lied about her connection to Nancy Jacobs and the group that tried to take me down with the Christmas Party ad."

"How much did she contribute to them?"

"I don't know. I don't even know that she did. Donors are anonymous. But I know something is going on. Anne and Nancy were best friends in high school, the committee is the largest contributor to Anne's charity, and I know Anne downplayed her connection with Nancy and her committee. What I don't know is why."

He looked at Linda as if she might have an answer.

"Maybe," Linda said, "she's teaming up with her brothers and backing Grindell."

"That's what I keep coming back to, but it's inconsistent. She's been so helpful to the investigation, with her memory thing and all. Was it all just for show? Does she also want to boot me out of office? And why?"

A sedan with two occupants pulled into the parking space beside Linda's open passenger-side door.

Otto powered down the driver's window. "Hey," he said, his tone buoyant. "Let's get this party started."

"Okay," Hood said.

Linda came to the van's driver's side and sheltered her husband under the umbrella as their footsteps splashed in the parking lot. As Otto emerged from his sedan, he called out, "There're puddles everywhere. Hold on." He opened the back door and pulled form-fitting rubber galoshes over his shoes. Hood was reminded that James Bishop had been wearing overshoes when his body was found, but those were the clumsier, four-buckle variety. The sheriff circled an arm around Linda's waist, pulled her close, and whispered, "Let's find out if it's time to shout or cry."

The foursome entered the Lion's Den, where some department personnel and supporters already had gathered for the watch party. Hood weaved his way among the tables, accepting handshakes, hugs, and encouraging words from well-wishers as he worked his way to the table Otto had reserved.

Hood and Otto moved chairs so all four could watch the big-screen television where local news anchors were reporting and assessing early returns.

A waitress appeared at the table and everyone ordered drinks—a ginger ale for Hood and three draft beers.

The votes from the precincts remained fairly even, see-sawing back and forth as Hood and Grindell exchanged the lead.

Hood heard a few rumblings of unease that began to spread like a contagion among his supporters. He knew better than to stay until it infected him as well. "Excuse me," he said. He stood and exited through the front door.

Outside, he sheltered under a large awning as the night sky and evening breeze replaced the closeness of the crowd indoors. His mood lifted, but only slightly. He reminded himself, for the umpteenth time, to avoid expectations because they may lead to disappointments and resentments.

A couple approached, walking arm in arm, along the

sidewalk. At the door, the woman extinguished a cigarette in the outdoor ashtray of the restaurant, where smoking was prohibited by city ordinance.

Hood contemplated how smoking a cigarette would be perfect for a time like this. He had given up smoking years ago, when the habit became inconvenient and smokers became pariahs in public.

A virtue of smoking, however, was it created the appearance of activity—doing something or taking a break from doing something.

Instead of simply standing outside the Lion's Den, buffeted by some stream-of-consciousness chaos, he at least would be smoking a cigarette, or—as a smoker might proclaim—enjoying a smoke.

His musings were banished abruptly when Otto emerged outside.

"Needed some air, huh?" Otto asked, as he stood beside Hood on the sidewalk.

Hood nodded. "I was getting a little uncomfortable in there."

"Well, it's starting to turn in your favor," Otto said, his tone reassuring.

"Looked pretty close to me."

"You're holding your own in the city," Otto said. "I figure if you win the city or even stay close, you win. You'll run stronger than Grindell out in the townships, in the county. You've got the edge there."

"We'll see," Hood said.

The sound of the door opening prompted both men to turn as Linda leaned outside and looked at them. "You two may want to come inside," she said. "The county returns are coming in quick, and they're coming in strong."

They followed her indoors and returned to their seats. As Otto predicted, the township results were updating rapidly with Hood garnering an ever-increasing majority that prompted rising exuberance and revelry in the restaurant.

Hood felt his cell phone vibrate and stepped outside again—this time to take a call from Grindell.

"Congratulations," Grindell said.

"Thanks."

"You earned the victory, Francis. The people have confidence in you."

"Thanks," he repeated.

"You're a good sheriff, Francis. Keep up the good work."

"I hope to. I mean, I plan—" Hood began, then stopped, unsure what to say.

"Well," Grindell said. "I won't keep you from your celebration." He disconnected.

Hood lingered on the sidewalk for several minutes before Otto summoned him to rejoin what had become a victory party, complete with champagne corks popping, streamers cascading, and the rhythmic chant of "speech, speech."

Unable to silence the clamor, Hood stepped on the elevated bandstand, stood at the microphone stand, and switched on the mic. "Thank you," he said, pausing to allow the applause and chatter to diminish. "Thank you. I'm truly humbled to be elected to serve as your sheriff for another four years, but—"

A crescendo of applause erupted, and again he paused until it began to fade. "But," he continued, "I didn't do this on my own." He looked at Linda. "I'm beginning to realize there are a lot of things I can't do on my own. And I'm beginning to understand that that's okay. It's okay to ask for help. I see now that it's not a sign of weakness. In fact, for me it's a sign of strength because it's the hardest thing I've ever had to do."

He scanned the family members, co-workers, friends, and supporters who had gathered, and an unexpected surge of joy and relief threatened to overwhelm him. "So thanks—all of you. Celebrate. Have fun."

He left the bandstand and again escaped outdoors. Moments later, Linda joined him.

"No champagne?" he asked her.

"I noticed you're not having any, either."

Hood smiled. "What I said in there, about needing other people—" He stopped, cleared the catch in his voice. "I kept telling myself I wasn't hurting anyone else, but I realize now—"

Linda put a finger to her husband's lips to silence him. "I understand," she said.

"I know this will take time," Hood said. "It's a process, but I want you to know I'm starting to feel different." He paused. "And I have a lot of people to thank for that—you particularly."

"You have no idea how much I appreciate that," Linda said. "Now let's go celebrate. This is your night."

CHAPTER 29

"Good morning," Maggie greeted. "How do you feel?"

"Relieved," Hood said. He poured morning coffee into a disposable cup.

"Me, too," she said.

"Why's that?"

"It's taken me nine years to get you broken in. I'm getting too old to start that again."

"You never know, Maggie. You may still be here long after I'm gone." He lifted the coffee pot. "Need a warmer?"

"Retirement doesn't appeal to me. I like what I do." She pushed her cup across the dispatcher's desktop. "What about you? You think you'll ever give it up?"

"Maybe if I stopped feeling like I was making a difference." He gazed into his cup momentarily. "Well, I've got four more years so I'd better get to work. I didn't get much sleep last night."

"Probably adrenaline from all the excitement."

"Truth be told, I haven't been sleeping well lately. This Bishop case has me tied up in knots."

"What's the problem?"

"I wish I knew. It's like something from the initial investigation doesn't fit with the new findings, but I can't put my finger on what it is."

"But you reviewed the original case file, right?"

"I reread my notes. They didn't help, but there wasn't much there—no crime, no evidence of foul play, alibis all around. I kept waiting for something to develop, but it never did."

"Until your daughter found the bone."

Hood nodded. "And when it was identified as James Bishop's arm, I hoped I'd be able to figure out what happened and finally give some closure to the family."

"And to yourself."

He nodded again. "But now I wonder if that's ever going to happen."

"Did you listen to the tapes again?"

"You mean from the initial interviews? No."

"Maybe they'll trigger something," Maggie said.

Hood shrugged. "Can't hurt." He refilled his cup and headed for his office, where he retrieved his recorder from a desk drawer before sitting in his chair.

He lifted the accordion folder from where he had left it atop a shelving unit, rummaged its contents, and removed five tapes. One tape—marked "Anne Bishop interview: Wallendorf"—reminded him he had listened to it only once, nearly a year ago.

He inserted the tape, pressed play, leaned back in his chair and listened.

The drone of the familiar voices repeating information he already knew created a rhythm that lulled him into a hypnotic dreamscape.

"According to your mother's description of what James was wearing that morning," Wally's voice intoned. "He had on a white polo shirt and khaki slacks. Is that your recollection?"

"Yes," Anne's disembodied voice answered.

"And," Wally added, "she said he might have been wearing a light blue windbreaker and overshoes he kept in his car."

"He had on both," Anne replied. "I call those overshoes his 'goofy galoshes' because they're those four-buckle boots and he tucks his pants into them."

Hood sat upright, nearly coming out of his chair as he snapped to attention. He pressed the stop button on the recorder, then rewind, then play.

The tape repeated: *"I call those overshoes his 'goofy galoshes' because they're those four-buckle boots and he tucks his pants into them."*

How, Hood wondered, did she know that? For that matter, how did Marjorie know what her husband was wearing?

Their descriptions were plausible at the time of the disappearance because the initial alibi was that James had left the house *after* the family members had gathered.

But once the alibi was withdrawn and everyone admitted James left the house before they arrived, how could any of them know what he was wearing?

Hood got to his feet and prepared to leave. He needed answers.

*****

"Congratulations," Marjorie said to the sheriff as Connie escorted him into the family room. His arrival had again been delayed at the front gate while the housekeeper apologized via the speaker for some problem activating the automatic opener.

"Thanks," Hood said. When he noticed Marjorie reach for the puppy sleeping in her lap, he added, "Please, don't get up. I don't want to disturb Danielle."

"Oh, all she does is sleep, but I guess there isn't much to do around here anyway."

Hood settled into an overstuffed chair across from her. "I hope I'm not wearing out my welcome," he said, his tone apologetic.

"Don't be silly. I get tired of rattling around in this big house all by myself. I mean, I've got Danielle, but she's a yapper, not a talker." She patted Danielle's head. "And Connie's here during the week, but her English isn't good and, besides, the children hired her to assist me, not entertain me."

"Well, I won't take much of your time," Hood said, as he repositioned himself in the chair. "I really just have one question."

She looked at him, attentive.

"After your husband's initial disappearance nearly a year ago, you gave a description of what he was wearing. I didn't think anything about it at the time because you said he left after the family had gathered. But if he left earlier in the morning and no one saw him leave, how could you know what he was wearing?"

"Oh, that," she said, as if the answer was simple. "I woke up while he was getting ready. I looked over and he was sitting in a chair in our bedroom tying his shoes. He already had on a white polo and his khakis, which he typically wears on Sunday when he—"

"Hello, again," Anne interrupted.

"Anne," Marjorie said, her surprise apparent. "What brings you here—twice in one week?"

Anne crossed to the sofa, stooped and kissed her mother on the cheek. "Can't I just stop by occasionally to visit my mother?"

Based on the conversation, Hood wondered if Anne's presence was more than coincidence. He suspected Anne may have instructed Connie to contact her if Marjorie received a visit—specifically, a visit from the sheriff.

"Sheriff," Anne said, turning to him. "What are you two talking about?"

Although the question seemed conversational, Hood detected wariness in her tone. "I'm glad you're here," he replied, evading her question.

"Why's that?" Anne sat on the sofa, beside her mother and Danielle.

"I have a question. I listened to the recording of your interview with Deputy Wallendorf after your stepfather disappeared. He asked you to confirm your mother's description of what James was wearing and you did. You also said he was wearing the blue windbreaker and the buckled overshoes. I believe you called them his 'goofy galoshes.'"

She shrugged. "So?"

"So, if James left the house that morning before you arrived, how could you know what he was wearing?"

Hood noticed her hesitation, several beats too long, before she answered. "I just guessed. I just assumed he was wearing whatever Mother said he was wearing."

"But," Hood said, "your mother didn't say he was wearing the windbreaker and the galoshes. She said he kept them in his car."

"I don't see what any of this had to do with anything," Anne said, clearly unnerved. She stood. "I've got places I need to be." She walked briskly from the room.

When she was gone, Marjorie said, "What was that all about?"

"I think I'm wearing out my welcome with your daughter."

CHAPTER 30

Hood was driving along a county road when his ring tone sounded. He activated the hands-free feature, glanced at the dashboard display, and said, "Hello, Anne."

"Sheriff, meet me where my stepfather's remains were found. Please come alone." The sound of the disconnection reverberated in the cruiser's interior.

He changed direction and headed toward Schoolhouse Road while questions and concerns collided in his mind.

Did she mean the Trestle site or the actual crime scene? As far as Hood knew, Anne was never told where the remains were found. Why did she ask him to come alone? Did she want a private conversation? Should he take precautions?

He activated his phone and called Maggie. "Just so you know," he told the dispatcher, "I'm meeting Anne in the area where James Bishop's remains were found."

"Should I send backup?"

"No. She asked me to come alone. I just wanted someone to know."

After they disconnected, he called Anne, but he was directed to voice mail.

He wondered, as he turned onto Schoolhouse Road, why she hadn't answered.

He bypassed the gravel road that led to the Trestle and continued on Schoolhouse Road until he saw Anne's silver BMW parked on the roadside facing the gated trail. This was the location where, days ago, Phil had waited by the four-wheeler to transport him, Loeffelman, and Sandra to the crime scene.

Hood parked on the roadside, exited the cruiser, and began the trek. He reminded himself to be cautious, but he didn't feel any sense of dread or jeopardy. Lately, Anne had seemed preoccupied, perhaps flustered, but he didn't know her well enough to guess what might be troubling her.

He crossed the dry creek, crested the knoll—where he guessed Wally had found the bullet casing—and approached the area where the remains had been found.

He was about to call her name when she startled him by stepping from behind a tree. She held the Heckler and Koch .45 mm handgun she had used at the gun range.

"Remember this?" she asked, displaying the weapon in a casual manner.

Hood nodded. Although he tried to remain outwardly calm, a surge of adrenaline already was elevating his heart rate and his breathing. "What are you doing with that?"

She put the gun barrel under her chin and pressed it against the soft underside.

Hood took a step, prompting her to point the gun at him. "Don't," she warned.

He stopped. He mentally calculated the distance between them and knew it was too far for him to intercede.

"I mean you no harm, Sheriff," she said. "This will be my last memory. It doesn't need to be yours."

Hood struggled to recall what little he had learned about dealing with suicidal subjects. The advice reverberating in his brain was to keep them talking. "I'm at a loss here, Anne," he said. "Tell me what's going on."

"What's going on is I know you know."

Hood watched pain cloud her expression as she closed her eyes. He was reminded of the common compulsion to wiggle a sensitive tooth or the alcoholic obsession to take another destructive drink. As he considered whether he could safely step forward, she opened her eyes. "What is it you think I know?" he asked.

"I know you suspect me. You may not be able to prove it. Maybe not yet, but I know you won't quit—not this time."

He waited a few beats for her to continue. When she didn't, he said, "Talk to me, Anne. Tell me about it."

"I can't deal with the memories anymore," she said. "They're eating me alive." Again, she closed her eyes, and Hood cautiously eased forward as he envisioned her reliving another place and time. "I've been invisible for so long," she added. "I've tried so hard to get him to see me, to notice me—ever since I was a little girl."

"Your stepfather?"

She nodded. "I wasn't a Bishop. I wasn't a son." She lowered her gaze and pursed her lips. Hood thought she was going to cry, but she raised her head, looked at him directly, and said, "I never knew my real father and when I finally got one—my stepfather—he couldn't even acknowledge me. It was like I was some novelty with a freak memory, so he stashed me in the accounting department like some crazy relative who lives in the attic."

She stopped speaking and again closed her eyes.

When they remained shut, Hood crept nearer, snapping a twig underfoot.

Anne's eyes flashed open. "That's far enough, Sheriff," she warned.

He stopped. "Did you shoot him?"

"I had to. Whenever I saw him, it triggered a memory. I felt the pain all over again. I used Jay's gun. You probably guessed that."

"So your plan was to implicate your brother?"

She nodded. "It was a good plan. After Jay bought the military rifle, I went with him to the range to try it out. When he turned his back to reload, I used a pencil to pick up a bullet casing with his fingerprint and hung onto it. When Father said he planned to visit that development site before the Sunday dinner, I spent Saturday finding this place. Then, in the middle of the night, I swiped Jay's gun and hid it under some leaves on that rise over there." She pointed to the knoll.

"Sunday morning, I met Father at the site and told him I'd heard of another possible location. I suggested we take my car since I knew where it was. After we got here, I said I needed to relieve myself, walked over the rise, and retrieved the rifle. When it was done, I replaced the bullet casing with the one that had Jay's prints and waited for someone to find the body."

"But," Hood said, "no one did—at least, not right away."

"The best laid plans, right?" Anne said. "I also didn't expect Mother to come up with the alibi that we all were together. But it all worked out. Those horrible memories stopped. That was the main thing. I was able to move on and things seemed to be working out—that is, until you found the body and reopened the investigation."

Hood shrugged, trying to feign nonchalance as he shuffled a half-step closer to her.

Anne extended the handgun in a threatening manner. "And then Mother withdrew the alibi, which was fine, but I needed you to focus on Jay, so I swiped his rifle and ammo again and took a shot at you. It was an intentional miss, by the way. The only problem was I didn't have another casing with Jay's prints, so I wore gloves and wiped down the rifle before I put it back."

Anne stopped talking. She closed her eyes tightly, transported into another memory.

Disturbed by the silence, Hood stepped forward and said, "Please give me the gun, Anne. We can—"

"No." Her eyes opened wide. "We can't. I can't. When he was gone, the memories disappeared. But now I have a new memory—the look on his face when he saw me in the instant before I pulled the trigger. My stepfather was more than surprised, he was indignant. It was like how dare I do something like that to him. And since his remains were found, that's what I see, that look, over and over. I can't live with it anymore." Her hands shook violently—her entire body quaked—as she put the gun under her chin.

"I can't let you do this," Hood said.

He stepped closer and, again, she removed the gun barrel from under her chin and began to level it toward him.

In that moment, he lunged at her, feeling the sharp sting and radiating pain in his shoulder before he tackled her to the ground.

CHAPTER 31

Elizabeth rushed through the door of her father's hospital room, trailed by Linda.

From his reclining position, Hood extended his free arm and hugged his daughter for a long time. He swallowed and restrained a tear as they disengaged.

Linda stepped in and embraced him more carefully. "You gave us quite a scare," she said as she straightened.

"It's a superficial wound," Hood said, downplaying the injury.

"Nonsense," Linda said. "You could have been killed."

Hood knew she was right. Although Anne had no intention of killing him, his headlong rush at her could easily have caused an errant, fatal shot. "Well," he said, "you two are stuck with me. I'll be out of here tomorrow."

"And," Linda said, "I'll see that you follow doctor's orders. No racing out the door the first time you hear a siren."

Hood smiled at her as his chief deputy appeared in the open doorway.

Wally cleared his throat and said, "Hope I'm not interrupting."

"Not at all," Linda said. "We were just visiting." She turned to Elizabeth. "Why don't we go to the cafeteria and have some ice cream?" she suggested. "I'm sure your father has some questions for Wally."

After they left, Wally offered an update. "Anne's being held for the murder of her stepfather and assault with a deadly weapon for wounding you," he said. "She's on suicide watch, based on your account of what happened out there. The prosecutor is considering additional charges relating to the shooting at the gun range and the theft of her brother's rifle, but those can wait."

Hood nodded.

"Anything I can do?" Wally asked. "Anything you need?"

"Just keep the place running until I get back."

"Maggie's pretty much got that covered. By the way, she'll be stopping by as soon as her shift is over."

Hood nodded.

"Well, I'd better get going." Wally walked to the doorway, stopped, and turned back. "You know—" he began, leaving the sentence unfinished.

"Yeah, I know," Hood said.

"Okay."

After Wally left, Hood raised the bed slightly so he was propped at a steeper angle. He closed his eyes. Although he didn't want to indulge in self-reflection, something about being shot needed to be processed. In that moment, he felt blessed—for his family, his coworkers and friends, his recovery. He had been given the gift of grace—which he had heard defined as unmerited favor. The gift had nothing to do with what he deserved or what he had earned. It could not be paid back. For him, the only way to acknowledge it was to be grateful.

He opened his eyes and saw Kim standing in the doorway, holding a bouquet of flowers. She approached. "These are for you," she said. "They're forget-me-nots."

Hood hadn't known the name but recognized the species—soothing blue petals with yellow centers—as the flowers Anne had plucked while walking with him near the Trestle. He accepted the bouquet, inhaled the fragrance, then looked into Kim's eyes. "How are you?" he asked.

"I'm clean. Eight days, but who's counting?"

"You look good," he said. He was sincere. Her eyes had brightened, the gauntness had diminished, and some color had replaced the pallor.

"Thanks. I'm feeling better."

"That's what it's all about. If life didn't get better in recovery, no one would stick with it."

"It's hard, though. I still want to use."

"The obsession will go away."

"When?"

"From what I'm told, there's no magic number. It's different for different people. I know it sounds trite, but that's why they say take it one day at a time."

A silence ensued. Hood sensed Kim was uncomfortable.

Finally, she said, "I don't think I thanked you for saving my life."

Hood didn't know how to respond, so he said nothing.

"I mean," she continued, "not just for that, but for giving me a second chance."

"Thank you," Hood said.

"For what?"

"For taking it."

THE END

Acknowledgements

For me, nostalgia accompanies aging.

During my 70 years, I have experienced much grace and I am grateful for my family and countless valued friendships—from childhood, high school, college and graduate school, throughout my career and into retirement.

This book is dedicated to my parents. Previous novels have been dedicated to my sister, Carol, my wife, Kristie, and my adult daughters, Heather and Jane. All have provided enduring love and support.

Without specifying titles or how the following people helped with "The Forget-Me-Knot," I would like to thank Anji Gandhi, Madeleine Leroux, Randall Haight, Greg Markway, Will Randle, Greg White, Steve Wright, and Nancy Jakubowsky Yuzuik.

I am fortunate to partner with three wonderful editors at Cave Hollow Press. G.B. Crump, Rose Marie Kinder, and James Taylor are insightful readers who consistently offer suggestions that improve my manuscripts.

I also appreciate my fellow authors who have shared with me at writer's conferences, answered my questions, and contributed blurbs for my books.

In addition, thanks to the book sellers, librarians, educators, and readers everywhere who promote literature and the love of reading.

About the Author

Richard F. McGonegal is the author of three Sheriff Francis Hood mysteries published by Cave Hollow Press. *Sense of Grace* was published in June 2020, followed by *Ghoul Duty* in February 2022. The unpublished manuscript of *The Forget-Me-Knot,* the third in the series, was honored as second runner-up at the 2021 Killer Nashville Claymore Awards.

In addition, 24 of his short stories have been published, including nine in *Alfred Hitchcock's Mystery Magazine*. Four of those nine have been reprinted in anthologies. He is an active member of Mystery Writers of America.

McGonegal retired in 2017 as an editor for the News Tribune Co. in Jefferson City, MO., where he worked for more than 40 years.

He received a Bachelor of Arts degree in 1969 from Rutgers University, New Brunswick, N.J., and a Master of Arts degree in 1973 from the University of Virginia, Charlottesville. Both degrees are in English literature and language.

He and his wife, Kristie, live in Jefferson City and are the parents of two adult daughters, Heather and Jane.

www.ingramcontent.com/pod-product-compliance
Lightning Source LLC
Chambersburg PA
CBHW030807210726
48290CB00002B/462

9781734267822